DRAGON BALL

The Adventure Begins!

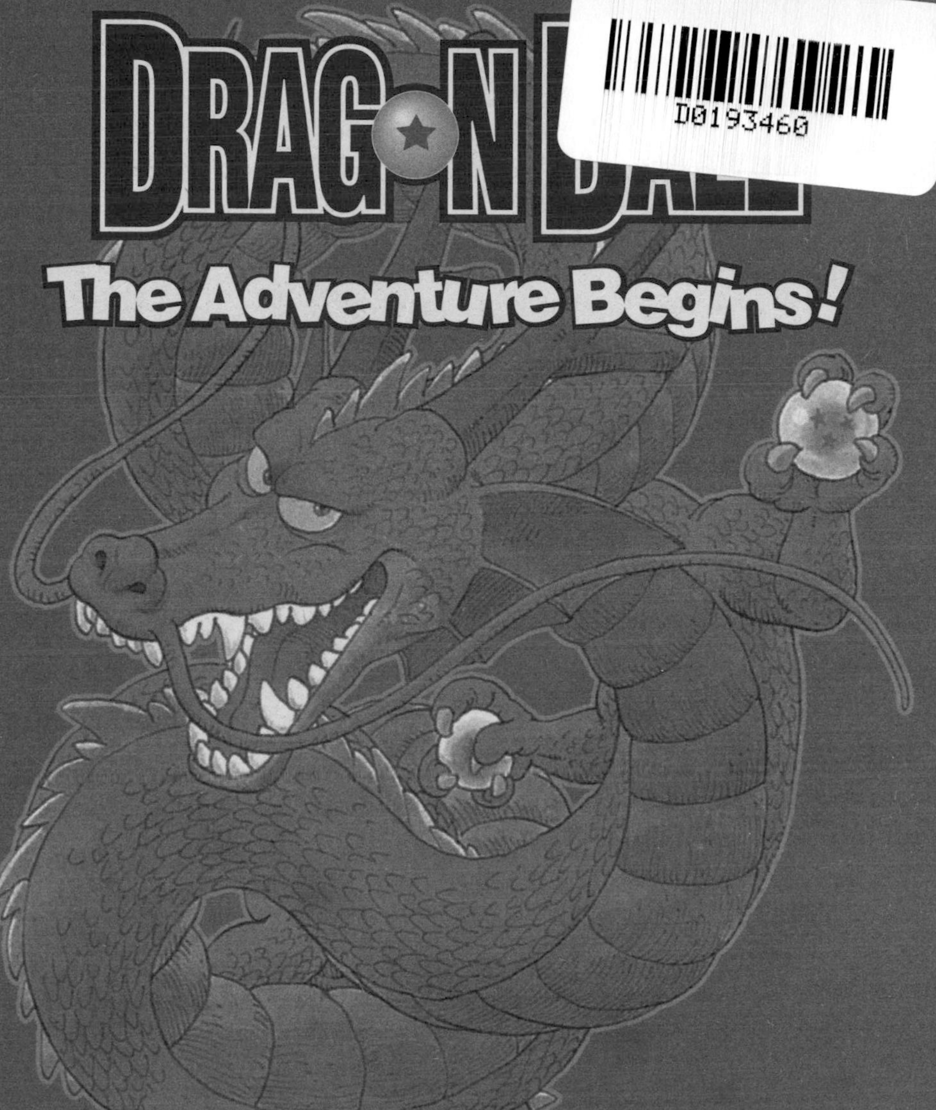

Based on the original story by **Akira Toriyama**

Adapted by Gerard Jones

DRAGON BALL THE ADVENTURE BEGINS
CHAPTER BOOK 1

Illustrations: Akira Toriyama
Touch-Up: Frances O. Liddell & Walden Wong
Coloring: ASTROIMPACT, Inc.
Original Story: Akira Toriyama
Adaptation: Gerard Jones

DRAGON BALL © 1984 by BIRD STUDIO. All rights reserved.
Original manga first published in Japan in 1984 by SHUEISHA Inc., Tokyo.
This English language chapter book novelization is based on the original manga.
The stories, characters and incidents mentioned in this publication are
entirely fictional.

Sources for page 78 "A Note About the Monkey King":

Julie Kulik, Kaijia Gu and David Patt, "Adventures in Chinese Culture: The Monkey King's Guide,"
East Asia Program at Cornell University
http://www.einaudi.cornell.edu/curriculum/monkey/journey/index.asp?grade=3
(accessed February 5, 2009)

Wikipedia contributors, "Sun Wukong," *Wikipedia, The Free Encyclopedia,*
http://en.wikipedia.org/wiki/Sun_Wukong
(accessed February 5, 2009)

Printed in the U.S.A.

Published by
VIZ Media, LLC
P.O. Box 77010
San Francisco, CA 94107

10 9 8 7 6 5 4 3 2
First printing, August 2009
Second printing, December 2018

www.vizkids.com   www.viz.com

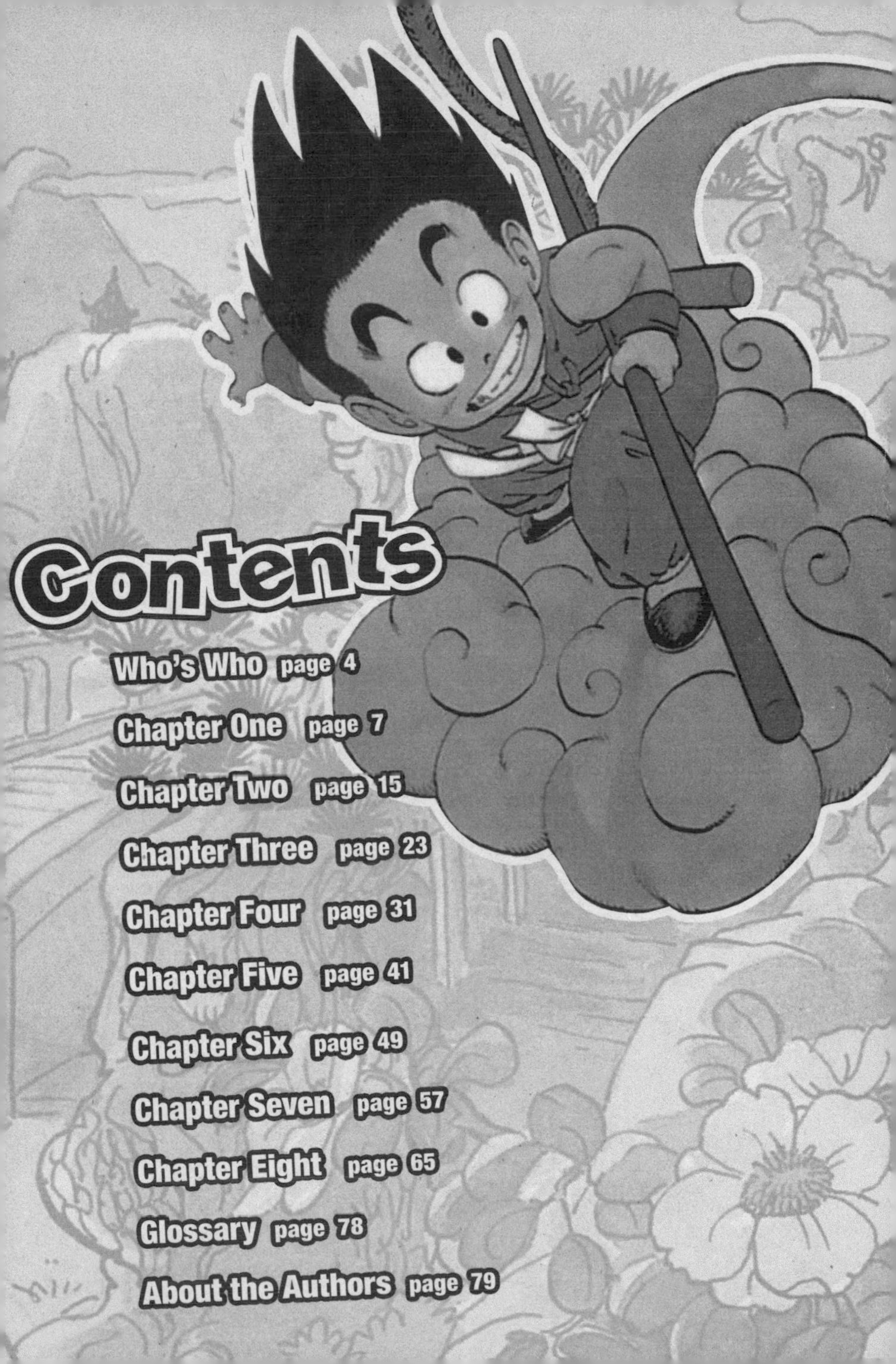

Contents

Who's Who

Goku

Since the death of his grandfather, Goku has lived alone, deep in a forest completely cut off from the wide world. He's small for his age but unnaturally strong. And what's with that tail?

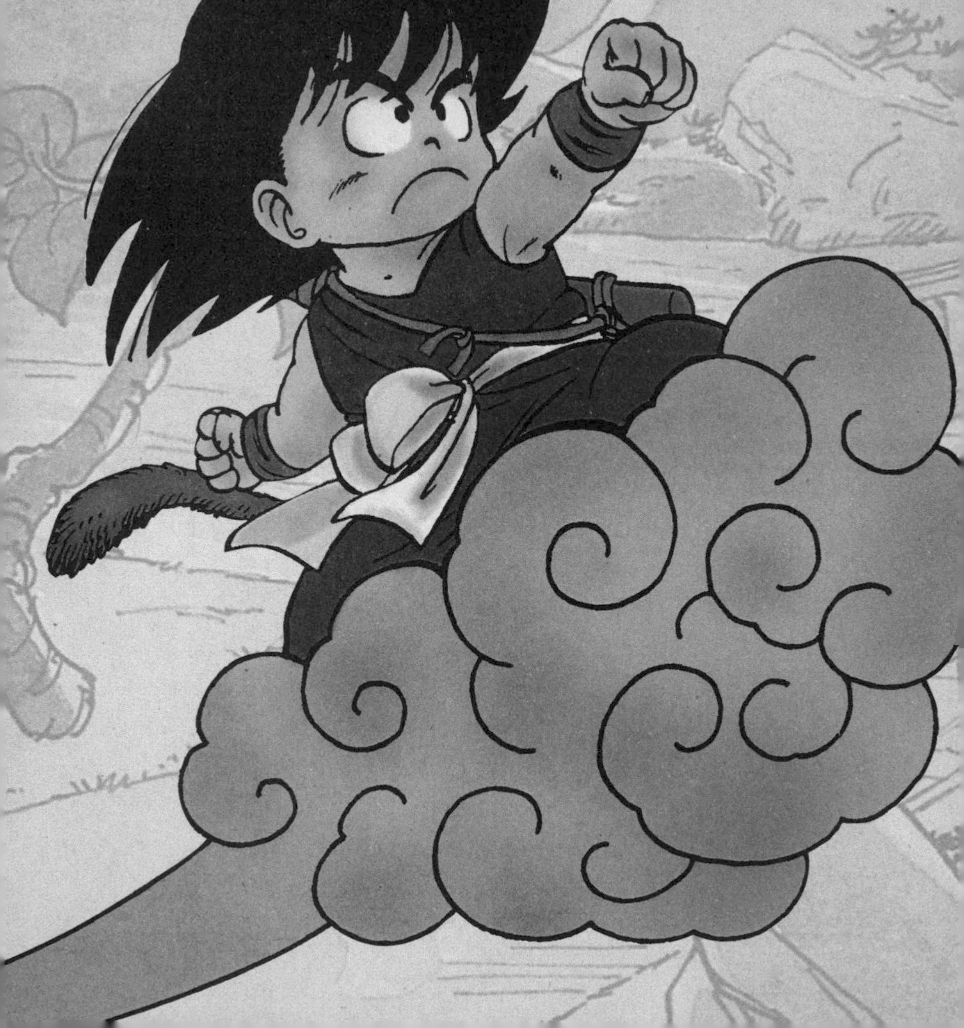

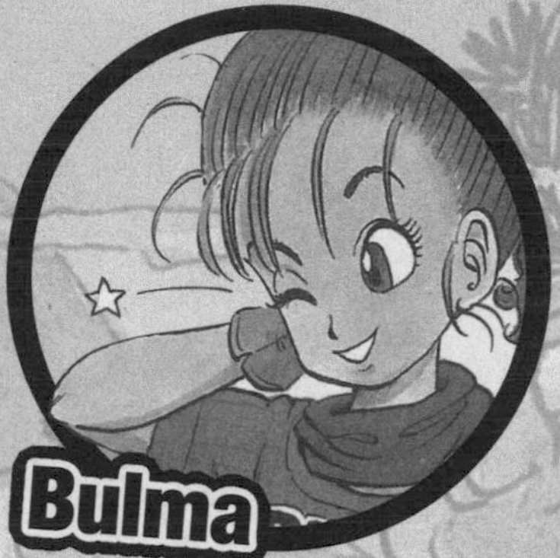

Bulma

Bulma's from the wide world and a technological genius. She's also a little hung up on her looks, but nobody's perfect. Besides, without her Goku'd still be hanging out in the forest, catching fish with his tail.

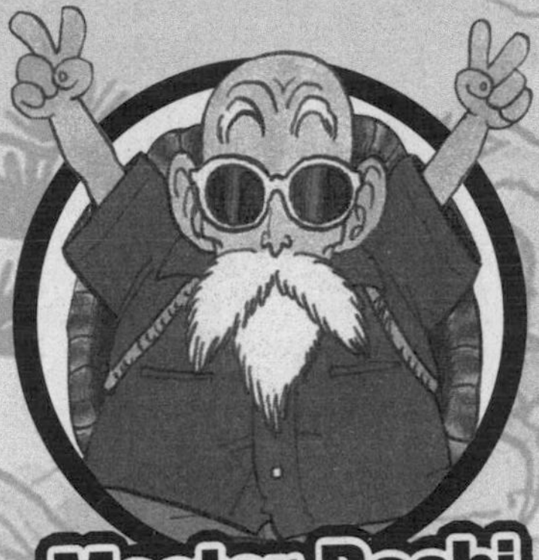

Master Roshi

a.k.a. Turtle Guy

Who is this guy with the magic cloud and the way with reptiles? All will be revealed in due time, but there's definitely more to him than meets the eye.

The Dragon Balls

Sushinchu
(soo-sheen-choo)
The four star Dragon Ball. Also known as the ball Goku's grampa gave him.

Ryushinchu
(ree-yoo-sheen-choo)
The six star Dragon Ball.

Oshinchu
(oh-sheen-choo)
The five star Dragon Ball.

Arushinchu
(ah-roo-sheen-choo)
The two star Dragon Ball.

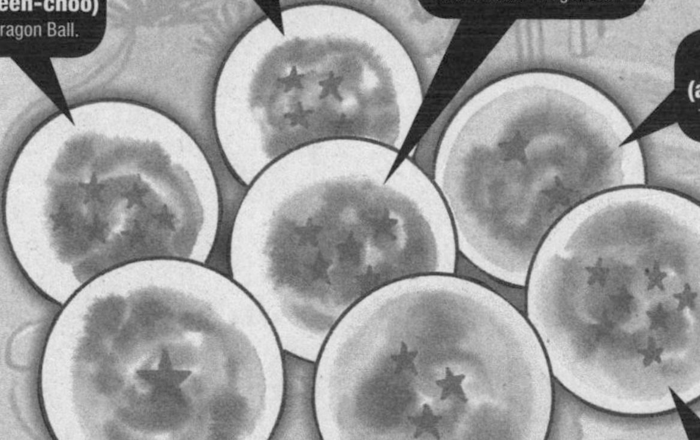

Chishinchu
(chee-sheen-choo)
The seven star Dragon Ball.

Isshinchu
(ee-sheen-choo)
The one star Dragon Ball.

Sanshinchu
(sahn-sheen-choo)
The three star Dragon Ball.

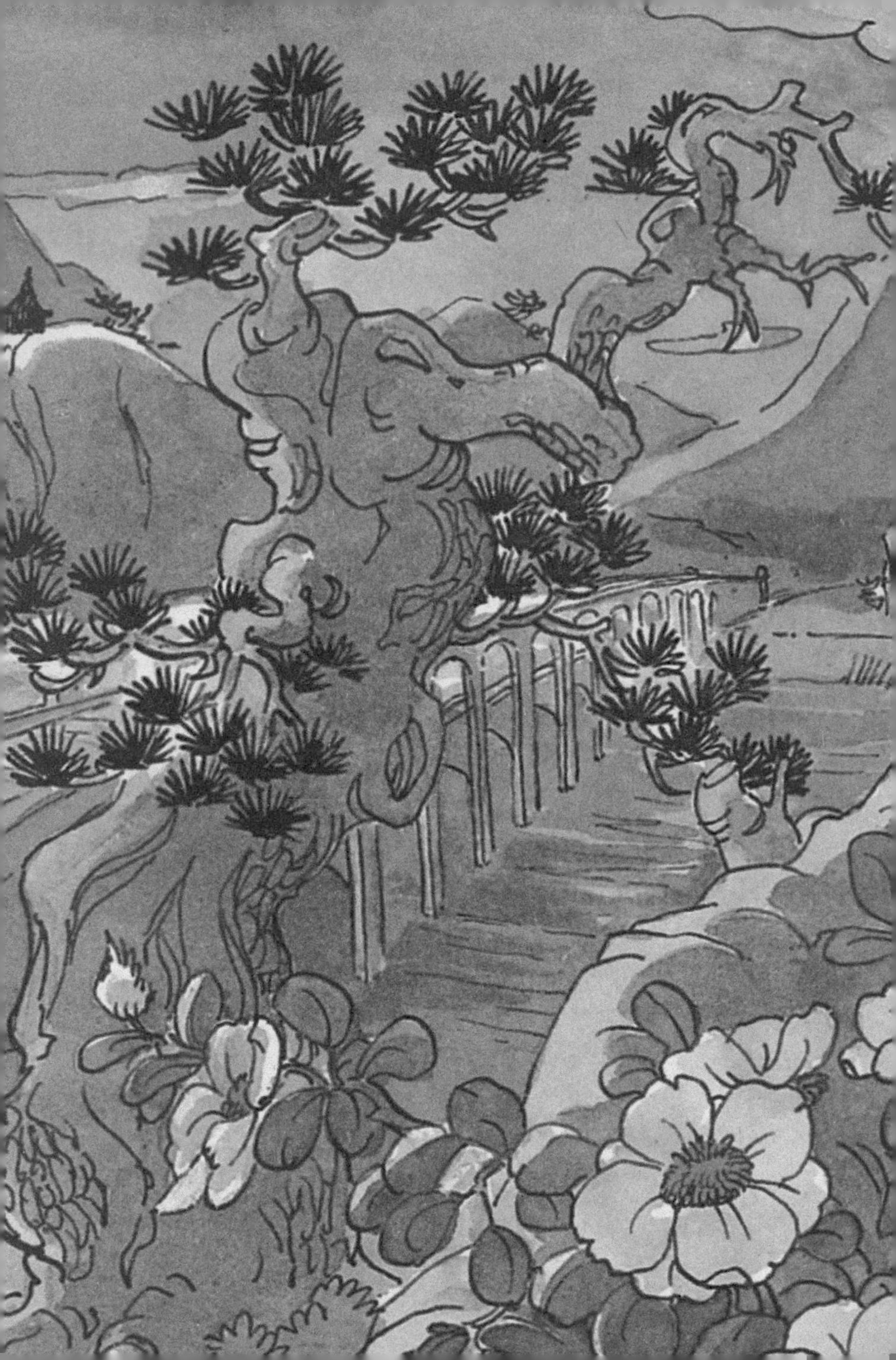

Chapter One

Deep in a dark forest far, far away from any town or road, Goku lived a simple life. He ate whatever he wanted, slept whenever he wanted, and trained to become as strong and fast as he could be.

His forest was full of wild things—monkeys and dinosaurs and bears—but Goku was perhaps the wildest thing of all.

On this morning, Goku rolled through the forest atop a thick log he'd just cut from a tree. The log was wider around than Goku was tall, but he had no trouble balancing on it as it zoomed through the brush like a runaway wheel.

"Chee! Chee!" cried a monkey as Goku whooshed by.

"Mornin'!" Goku replied, waving his tail hello.

When he got home, Goku jumped off the log. He circled it once, then crouched into a fighting stance.

"Prepare to die!" Goku cried, rushing at the log.

He wrapped his arms around it and heaved it high into the sky. Much higher than a boy his size should have been able to throw a log that big.

"There's no escape!" Goku called, and leapt into the air after the log.

He gave it a single mighty kick and the log shattered. Rough chunks of wood showered down to the ground.

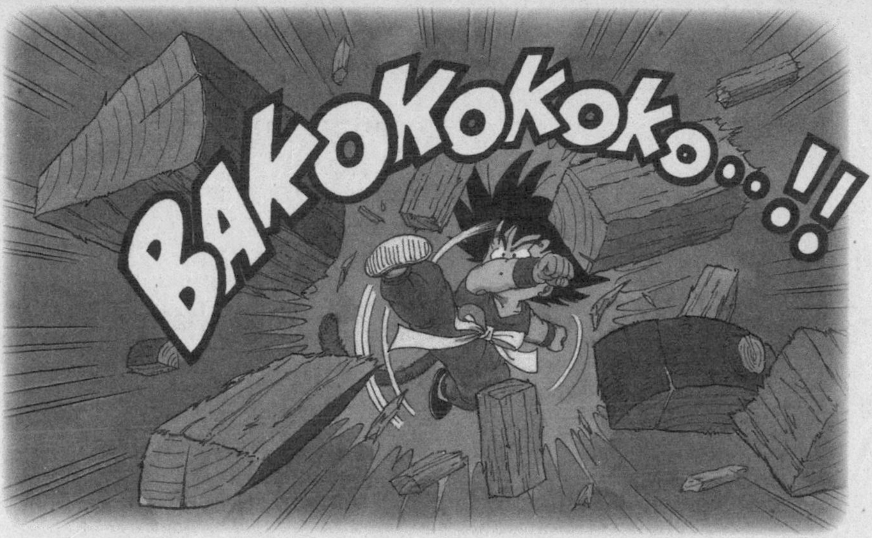
BAKOKOKOKO...!!

"Well," Goku laughed as he stacked the wood, "that takes care of the wood choppin'! Now I'm hungry!"

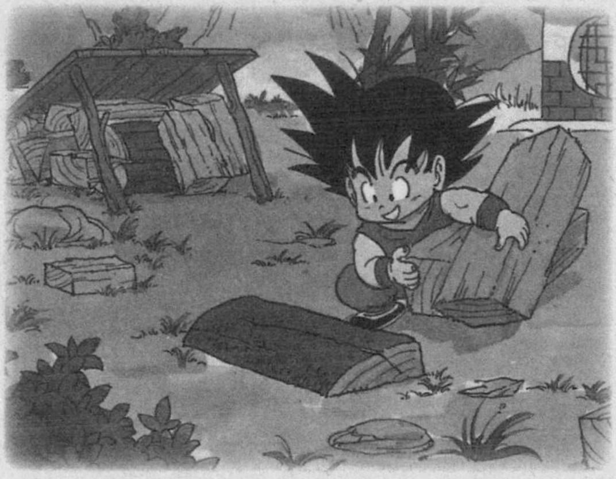

He went inside and tied his Nyoibo fighting staff to his back. It was time to hunt. But before he left, he knelt before a small shrine. On the shrine sat a crystal ball with four stars glowing inside.

"Hey, Grampa!" Goku said to the ball. "I'll be right back. I gotta get some grub!"

What should I eat? he wondered as he walked toward the deepest part of the forest. *Just had bear the other day... I wonder if I'll run into a tiger. Tiger would be tasty!*

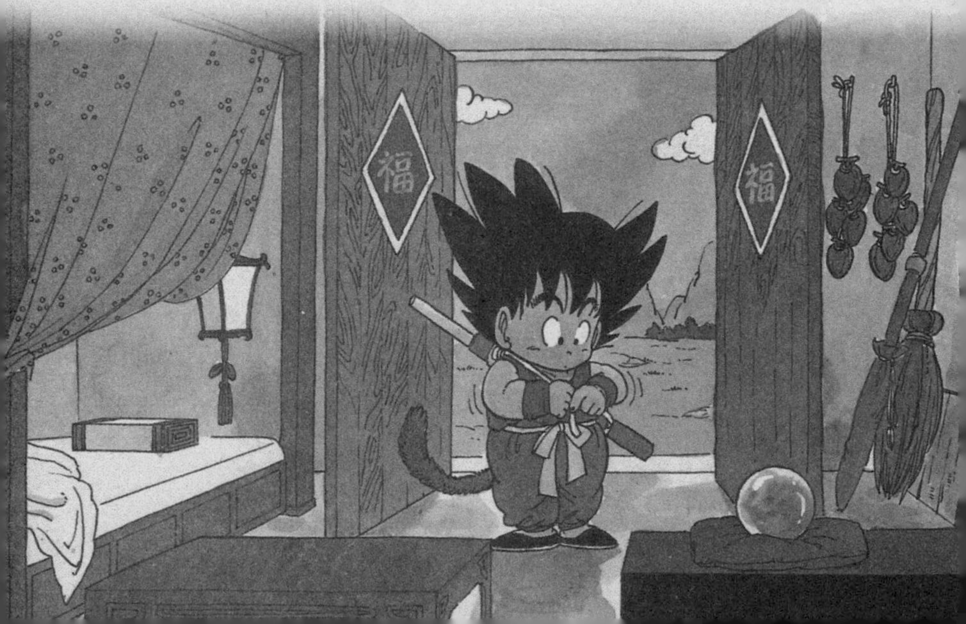
福
福

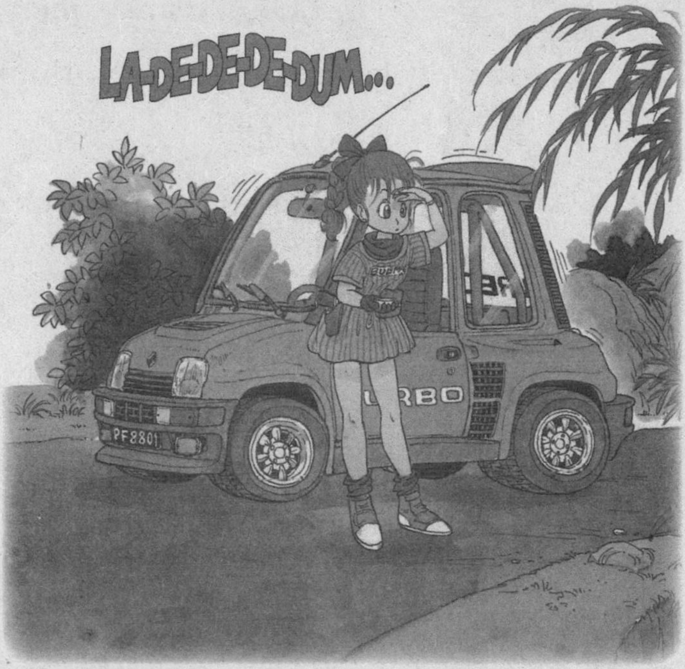
LA-DE-DE-DE-DUM...
PF8801

While Goku searched for food, a stranger entered the woods. She wasn't exactly dressed for exploring.

"It's got to be around here somewhere," she mumbled, looking at a beeping thing in her hand. "Maybe it's a little more to the west. I'm so close!" And with that, she got in her car and drove off.

Meanwhile, Goku had come to the edge of a very steep cliff. Far below, a river roared among the rocks.

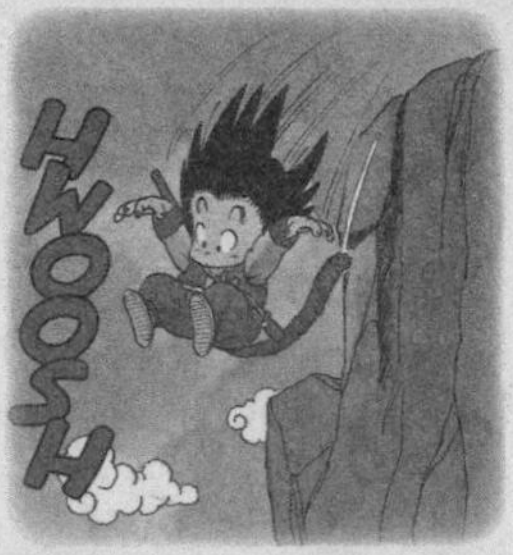
HWOOSH

"Oh yeah!" he said, looking down. "I think I'll have fish!"

And then Goku jumped.

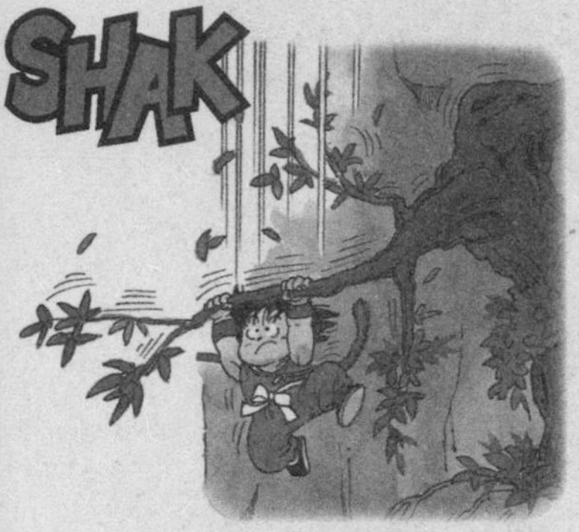
SHAK

Down, down, down he fell, swinging and vaulting from branches and tree roots.

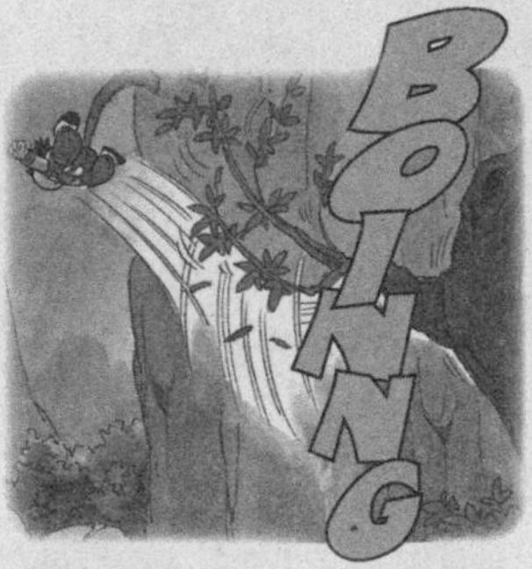
BOING

As the wind whistled through his hair, he let out a gleeful "Wheeee!"

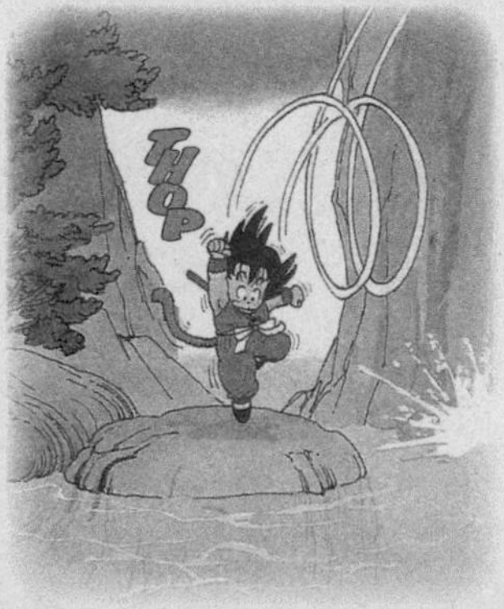
THOP

Finally, he landed at the river's edge with a very soft *thop*.

He took off his Nyoibo and placed it carefully on the ground. Then he peeled off his clothes, turned his backside to the river, and dipped his tail in the water. *Plip.* He lifted it up, then dipped it in again. *Plip.* He did this again and again until…

CHOMP!

…a fish more than twice Goku's size took the bait! It came flying out of the water after Goku's tail. While it was still in the air, Goku knocked it out cold with one powerful kick.

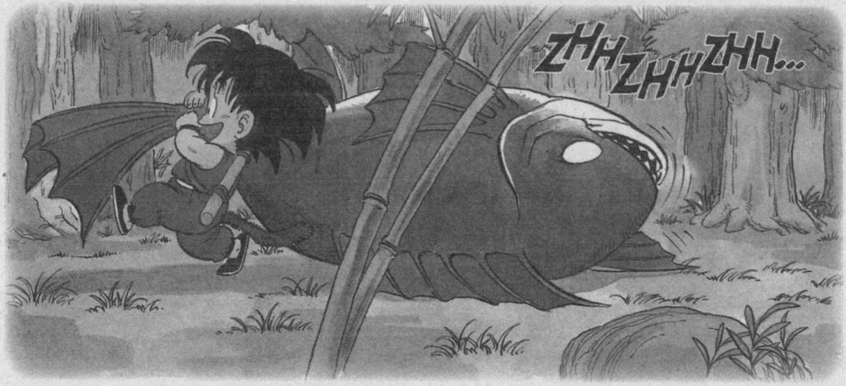
ZHH ZHH ZHH...

The fish sank deep into the river, and Goku dove after it. He dragged it to the surface and hauled it home.

"What a catch!" he sighed happily. "I can't wait to show Grampa!"

Suddenly, in the distance, Goku heard something like nothing he'd ever heard before. Like a growl with the roar of thunder thrown in. The louder the sound got, the more the ground shook beneath his feet. Something big was coming! It was getting closer. And fast!

Goku tossed the fish aside. He swung his staff from his shoulder and spread his feet wide. He was ready to fight.

When the thing burst from the trees, it was like nothing Goku had ever seen before.

"A *monster*!" he cried.

And it was racing straight toward him.

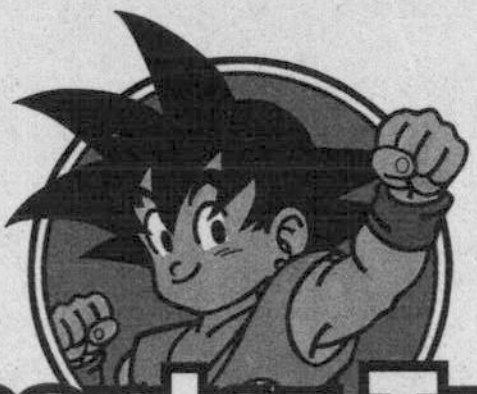

Chapter Two

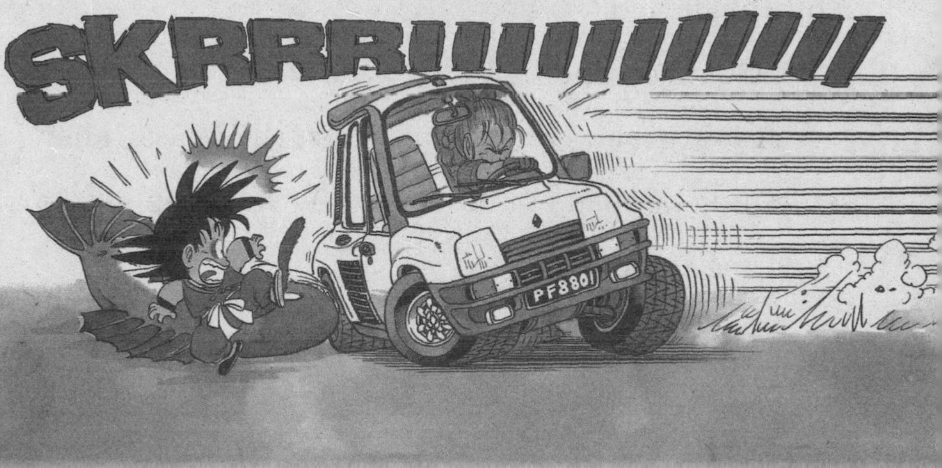
SKRRRIIIIIIIIIII
PF8801

The monster made a terrible screeching sound. It spewed dust and rocks as it bore down on Goku. At the last instant it turned, missing Goku by inches.

For a moment, Goku was stunned. But he quickly snapped out of it.

"Ha!" he laughed at the beast. "You call that an attack?"

He shimmied under the thing and lifted it over his head. "No way you're gonna steal my fish!" he yelled. He heaved the beast in front of him and sent it crashing to the ground. For a moment, all was quiet. Nothing moved.

"Come on and fight!" Goku called.

A low groan came from inside the beast. Then something popped out of its side. Goku snapped into a fighting stance.

“What are you?” he snarled, pointing his Nyoibo. “The hideous demon who controls the monster?”

“This isn’t a monster, it’s a *car*,” snapped the thing. “And who are you calling *hideous*?! Compared to you, I couldn’t *be* more beautiful!” The demon thought for a second. “In fact, I’m more beautiful than just about *anyone*!”

“I don’t care what you are!” Goku said, raising his staff. “You’re not stealing my fish!”

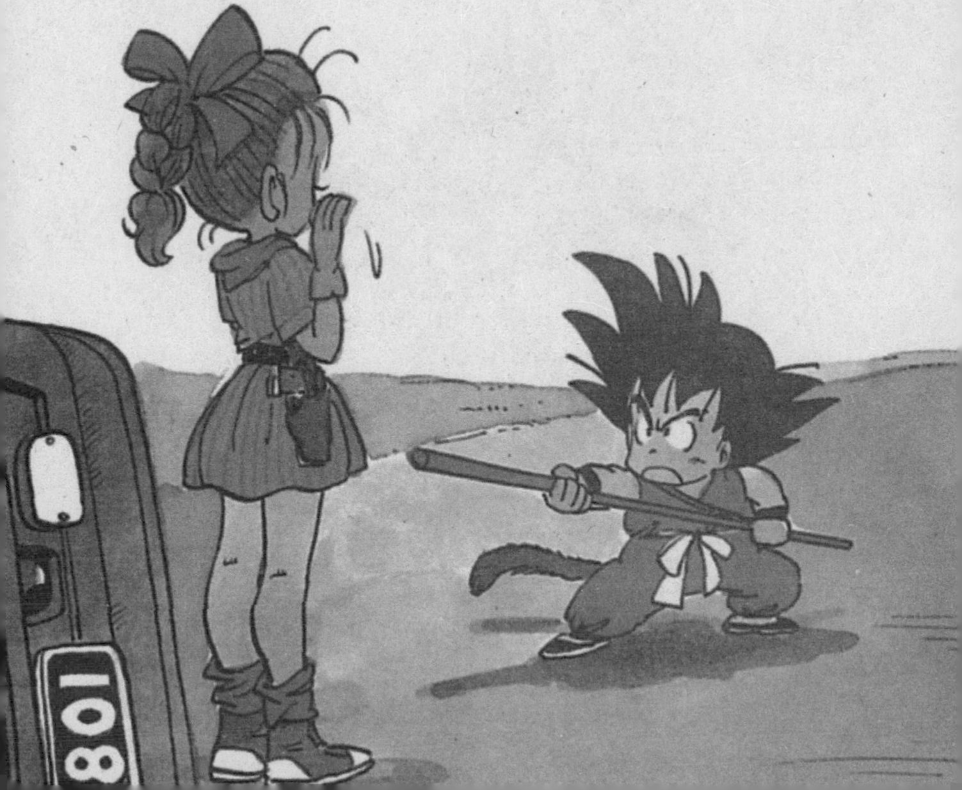

Then the creature laughed. It laughed and laughed and laughed. "You think I'd drive all the way from the city to steal a *fish*?"

"I don't know," Goku said. "What do demons steal?"

"We don't steal anything!" the creature said. "And I'm not a demon! I'm a girl!"

"A–a *girl*?" Goku gasped. "You mean—a *human*?"

"Duh. Haven't you ever seen a girl before?"

"I've never seen another human before," Goku said. "'Cept my grampa."

He walked around the girl, taking her in from all sides.

"You're not very trusting, are you?" she asked.

"Don't move," Goku replied.

Finally, he lowered his staff. "You're kinda like me," he declared. "But there's something different… Where's your tail?"

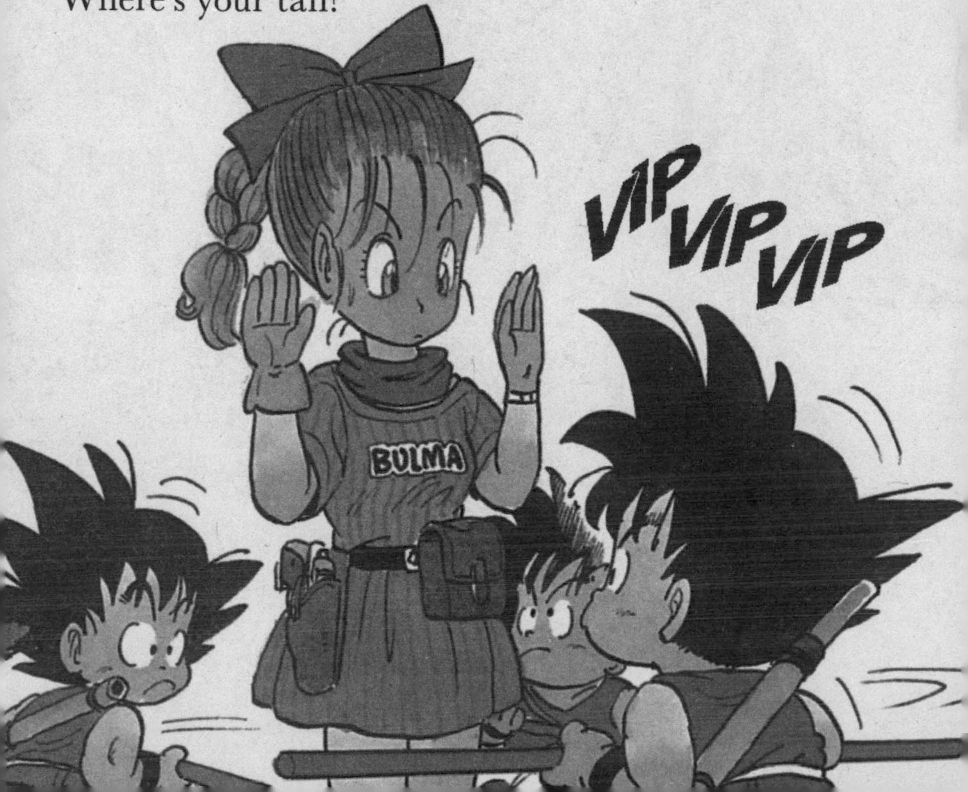
VIP VIP VIP
BULMA

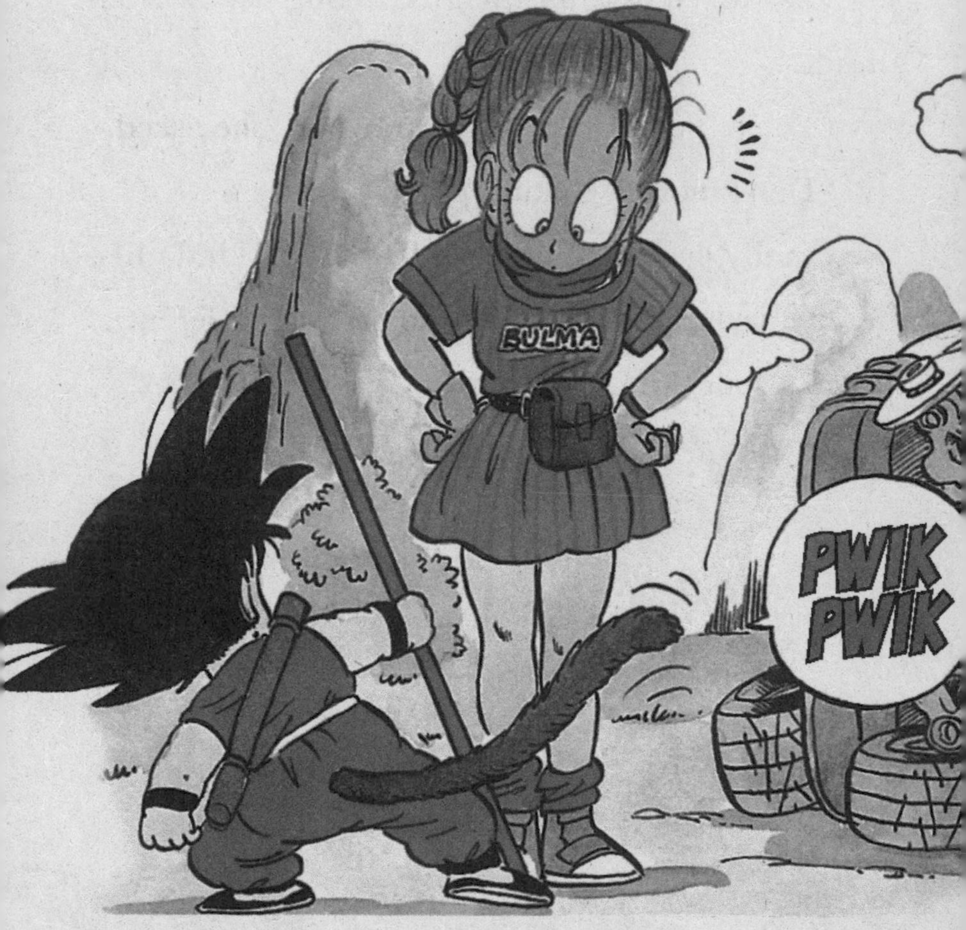
BULMA
PWIK PWIK

"What on earth are you talking about?" snapped the girl. "Humans don't have—" Goku waved his tail at her and waited.

The girl snickered. *Oh, man!* she thought. *He probably thinks that fake tail makes him look cool or something.*

"What kind of weirdo *are* you?" she laughed.

"I'm Goku!" he said brightly. "What kind of weirdo are *you*?"

"I'm...uh...Bulma. But that's not what I—"

Goku wasn't paying attention. Now that he was sure Bulma wasn't a threat, he wanted to inspect the thing that had first attacked him.

"So this is a car, huh?" he said, jumping on top of it. "Grampa told me stories about cars and all sorts of things from a place called *Civilization*. Is that where you're from?"

"Let's just say I'm from very, very far west," Bulma replied.

"Oh! Grampa also told me that if I ever met a

girl, I should treat her real nice," Goku said, remembering.

"Then don't you think you should get started? I'd like to meet this grandfather of yours!"

"Come on, then!" Goku said, grabbing her hand and leading her away. "I'll show him to you!"

Chapter Three

Goku opened the door to his house. "Grampa, look!" he yelled. "It's a girl!"

Bulma looked around for an old man who could be Goku's grandfather but didn't see anyone. Then she realized that Goku was talking to the crystal ball on the shrine. Her eyes grew wide.

"That's it!" she squealed. "The Dragon Ball!"

"Huh?"

Bulma shoved Goku aside and grabbed the crystal ball. "My radar was right! I knew it was here somewhere!"

"Hey!" Goku yelled, snatching the ball back. "Let go of that! Grampa left me that to remember him by! No one but me can touch it! Not even girls!"

"You mean," Bulma asked, "your grampa's dead?"

"Yeah," Goku said. "But talking to the ball makes me feel like I'm talking to him."

"Hmm…" Bulma said with a smile. "Maybe I should let you in on a little secret." She opened her purse and pulled out a crystal ball with two stars glowing inside.

"Another Grampa!" Goku cried.

As he watched, Bulma pulled out another crystal ball. This one glowed with five stars.

"*Two* more Grampas!" Goku breathed.

"No, no, silly. They're called Dragon Balls,"

Bulma explained. "A while ago I found the one with two stars in my cellar. I had no idea what it was, but I did some research and found an old, old story. Originally there were seven Dragon Balls, each with a different number of stars inside. The ones I have are called *Arushinchu*," she held up the two-star ball, "and *Oshinchu*, the five-star ball. And you've got *Sushinchu!*"

"*Sushinchu*," Goku breathed, looking closely at the four-star ball. "So you're collectin' these?"

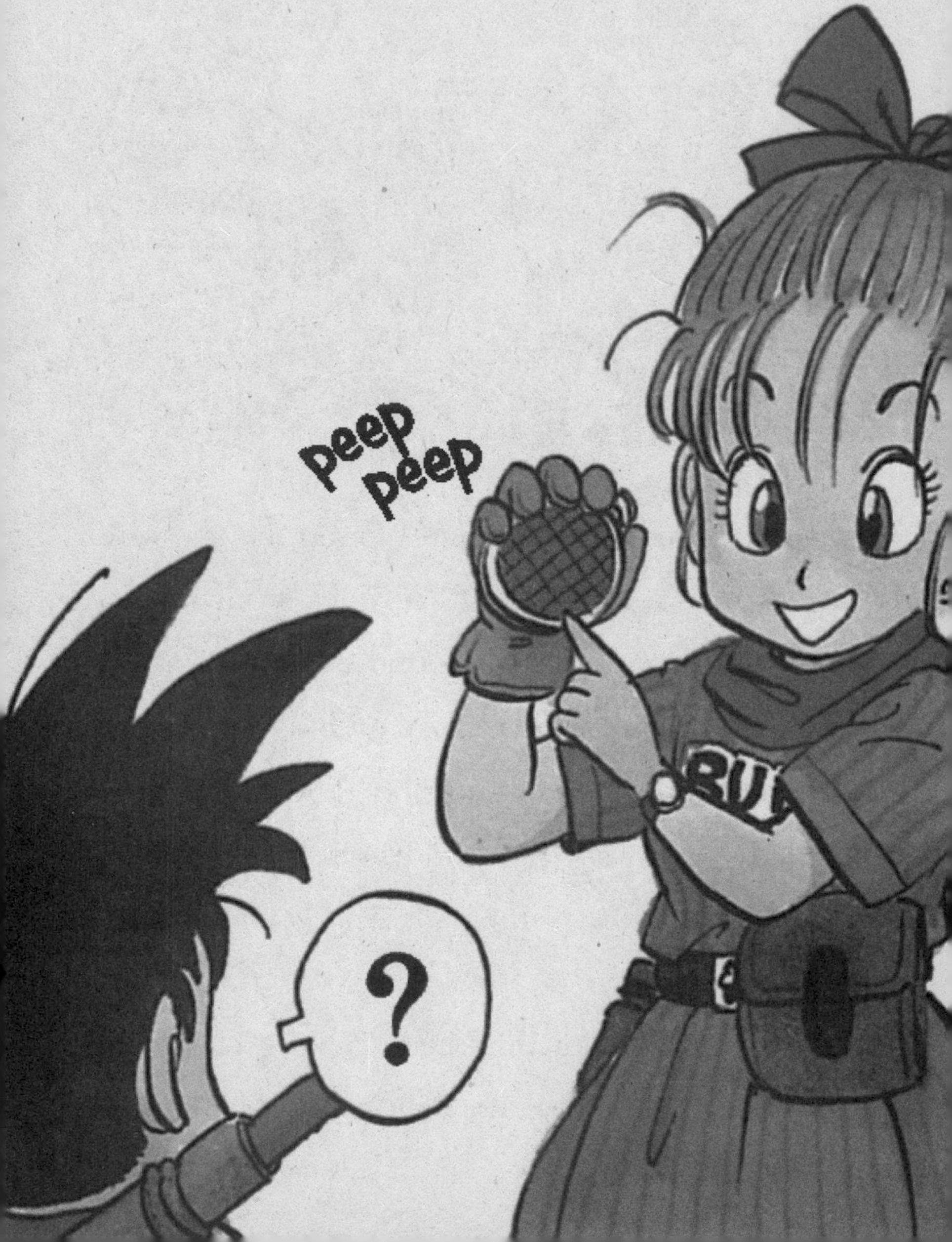
peep peep
?

"Yep! I even invented this!" Bulma pulled a strange gadget from her pack. "This is my Dragon Radar. It picks up the energy the balls give off. That's how I found your—um—grampa."

"What're you gonna do once you find 'em all? Make a necklace or something?"

"Very funny!" Bulma smirked. "When you have all seven Dragon Balls you can summon a dragon! He'll grant you any wish you want. The last person who found all seven became a king. Now the balls are scattered all over the world—but I'm going to find them and make my wish!"

"Are you gonna be a king?" Goku asked.

"Nah," Bulma said. "At first I wanted a lifetime supply of strawberries, but now I'm gonna wish for a really cute boyfriend!"

"I'd rather have the strawberries," Goku said.

"I'll send you some," Bulma said, "to thank you for helping with my quest!" And she grabbed the Dragon Ball off the shrine.

"Hey!" Goku yelled, snatching the ball back. "That's the only grampa I've got!"

"But I need all seven to make my wish," Bulma exclaimed. Then she smiled. "Oh, I get it! You want something in exchange!"

"I do?" Goku said.

"Uh-huh!" She leaned toward him. "You want a kiss!"

"A *kiss!*" Goku cried. "Why would I want your slimy lips on me?"

"My lips are not slimy!" Bulma snapped. "And any normal guy would give anything for a kiss from me!"

"So find one and put your lips on *him*!" Goku laughed.

"Fine," Bulma grumbled. "You win."

"I do?"

"Yes," Bulma said. "You can join my quest."

"Join your…quest?" Goku asked.

"You're big and strong, right?" Bulma asked,

looking him over. "Well, you're strong anyway, and strong guys love to be heroes!"

"They do?"

"Duh!" Bulma said. "We'll look for the other four Dragon Balls, and you can protect me when I'm in terrible danger!"

"Okay, I guess," Goku said. "But I'm not giving you Grampa!"

"Of course not!" Bulma said. "I'll just borrow him at the very end, to make my wish! Shall we go?"

And out the door they went.

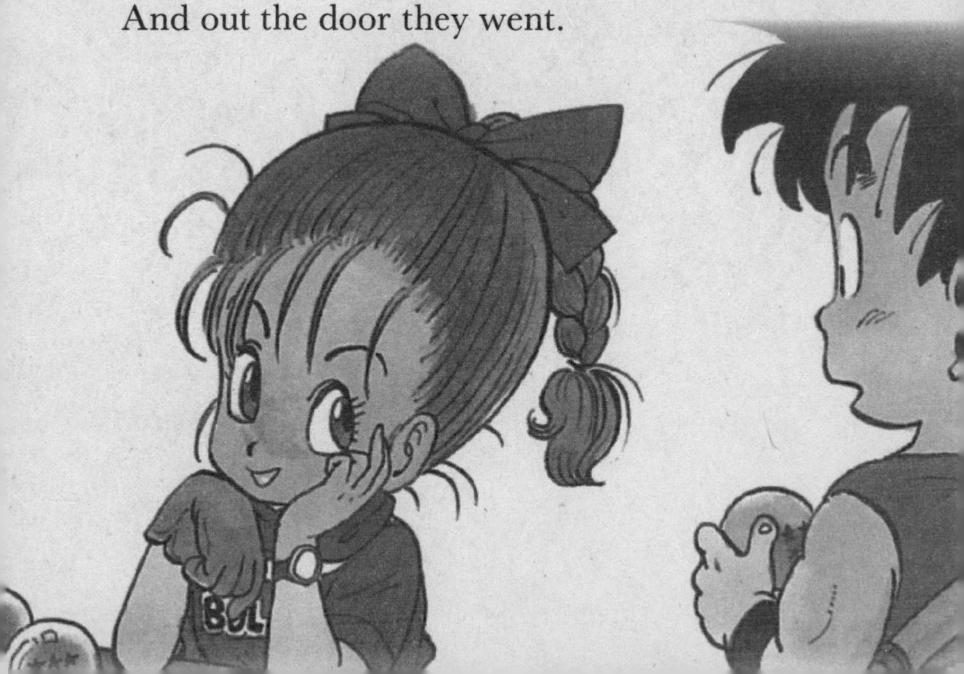

BUL

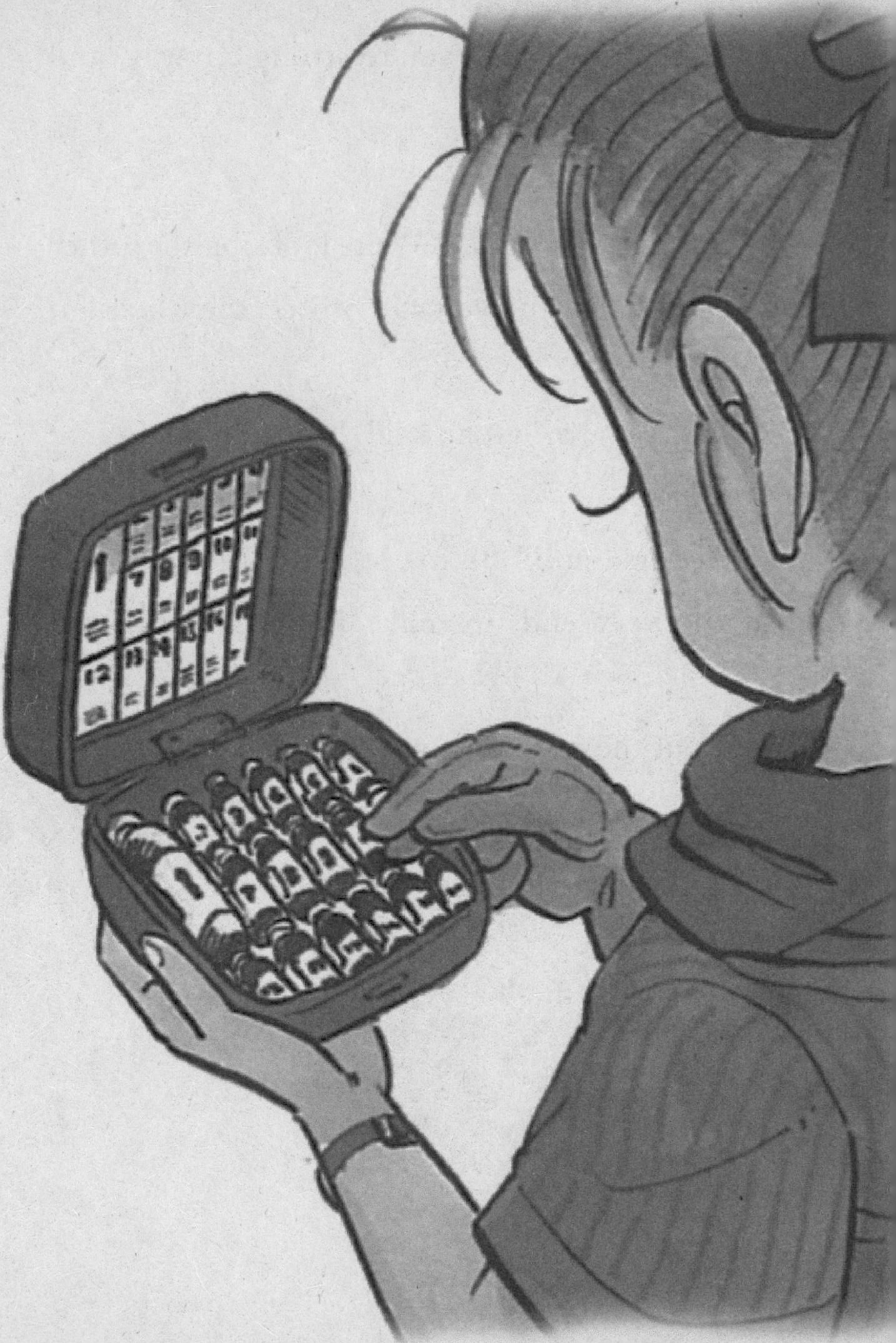

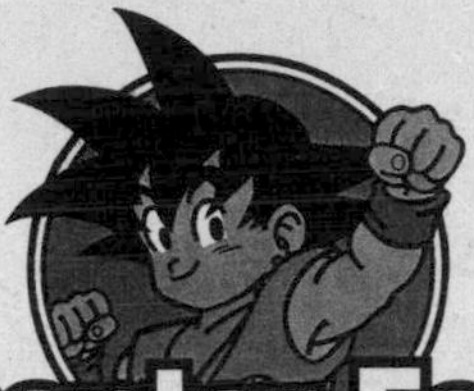

Chapter Four

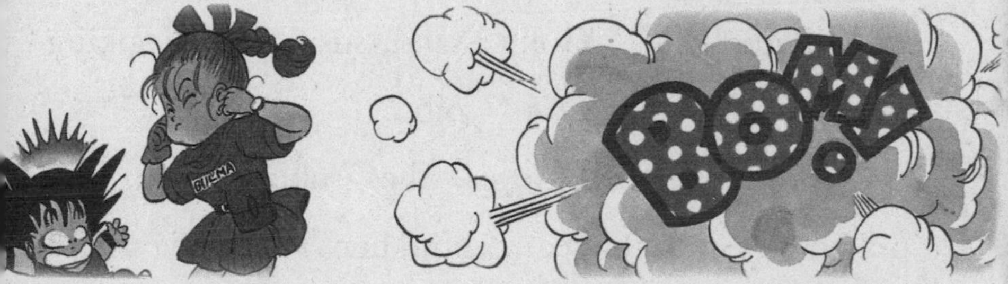
BOOM!

As soon as they were outside, Bulma took a strange little case out of her pack and opened it. The case was filled with small capsules, each with a number on it.

"Hmm," she said. "I guess I'll use Number Nine."

She threw the Number Nine capsule into the air. It hit the ground and exploded with a loud *boom*.

And when the dust settled, a motorcycle appeared.

"I knew it!" Goku yelled, jumping back. "You *are* a demon!"

"Oh, get over it!" Bulma said. "It's not magic. It's a Hoi-Poi capsule. Everybody in the city has them. Let's ride, already!"

"Ride what?" Goku asked, suspiciously poking the motorcycle with his Nyoibo.

Bulma rolled her eyes. She grabbed Goku and pulled him onto the seat behind her. Then she pushed a button and twisted the handlebar. The motorcycle roared and took off.

"Eee-yow!" Goku screamed. "It's running! It's running even faster than me! I didn't think *anything* could run faster than me!"

"Get ready to see a lot of things you never thought were possible!" Bulma laughed.

They started up a hill, and she made the motorcycle go even faster. It zoomed over the top with such speed that its wheels left the ground.

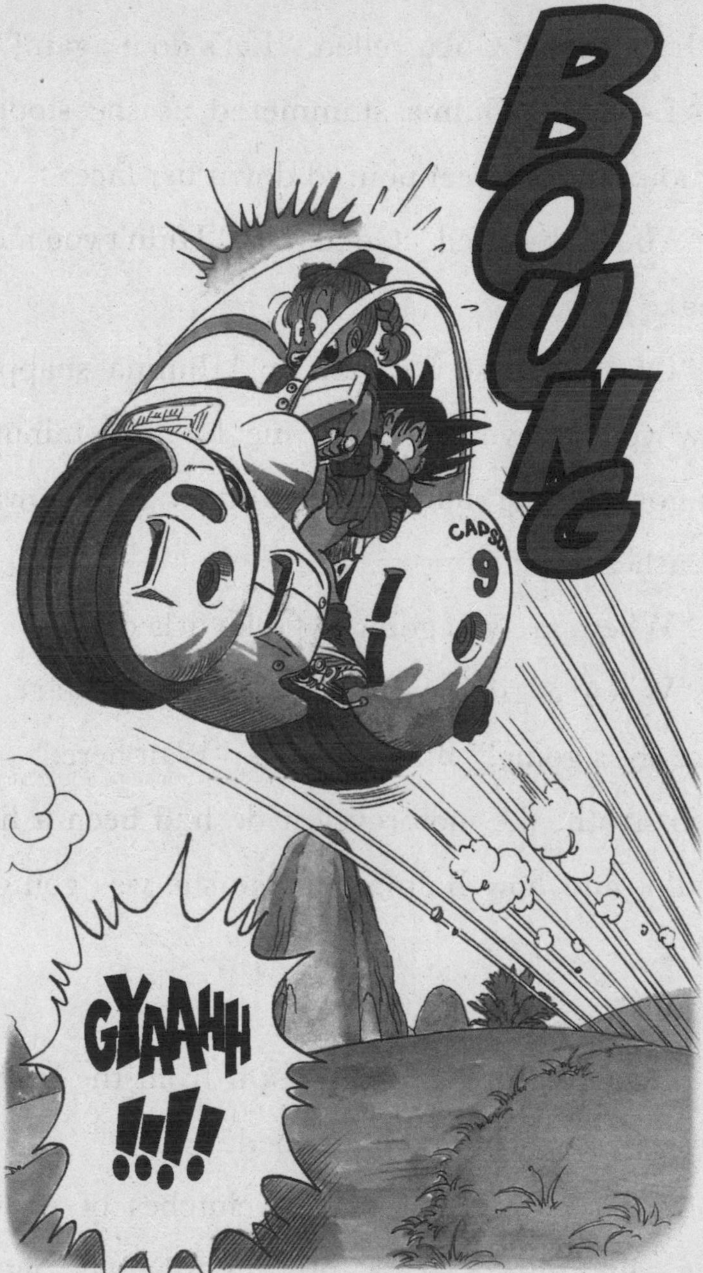
BOUNG
GYAAHH!!!!

It flies too!" Goku yelled. "Let's do it again!"

"L-l-later," Bulma stammered as she stopped the motorcycle. Sweat poured down her face.

"You look scared," Goku said. "Didn't you mean to make it fly?"

"Of c-c-course I meant to!" Bulma snapped. "Now you'll have to excuse me for a m-minute." She got off the motorcycle and walked toward the bushes.

"Where are you going?" Goku asked.

"When a girl says 'excuse me,' you don't ask where she's going!" Bulma yelled. "Wait here."

In truth, the motorcycle ride had been a little *too* wild, and now Bulma felt like she was going to be sick.

Goku waited.

Suddenly, he heard a scream from the bushes. He ran to see what had happened.

There was Bulma in the clutches of a huge flying dinosaur. Like a pteranodon but bigger.

Much, much bigger.

"Who are you?" the dinosaur snarled at Goku. "Part of her pack?!"

"No, I just met her," Goku said calmly. "Are you a friend of hers?" Goku looked at Bulma, but all she could do was scream.

The dinosaur thought for a moment, then cracked an evil grin.

"Yeah. That's it," he said, moving Bulma from his claws to his tail. "I'm a *friend* of hers." He grabbed a thick vine from a nearby tree.

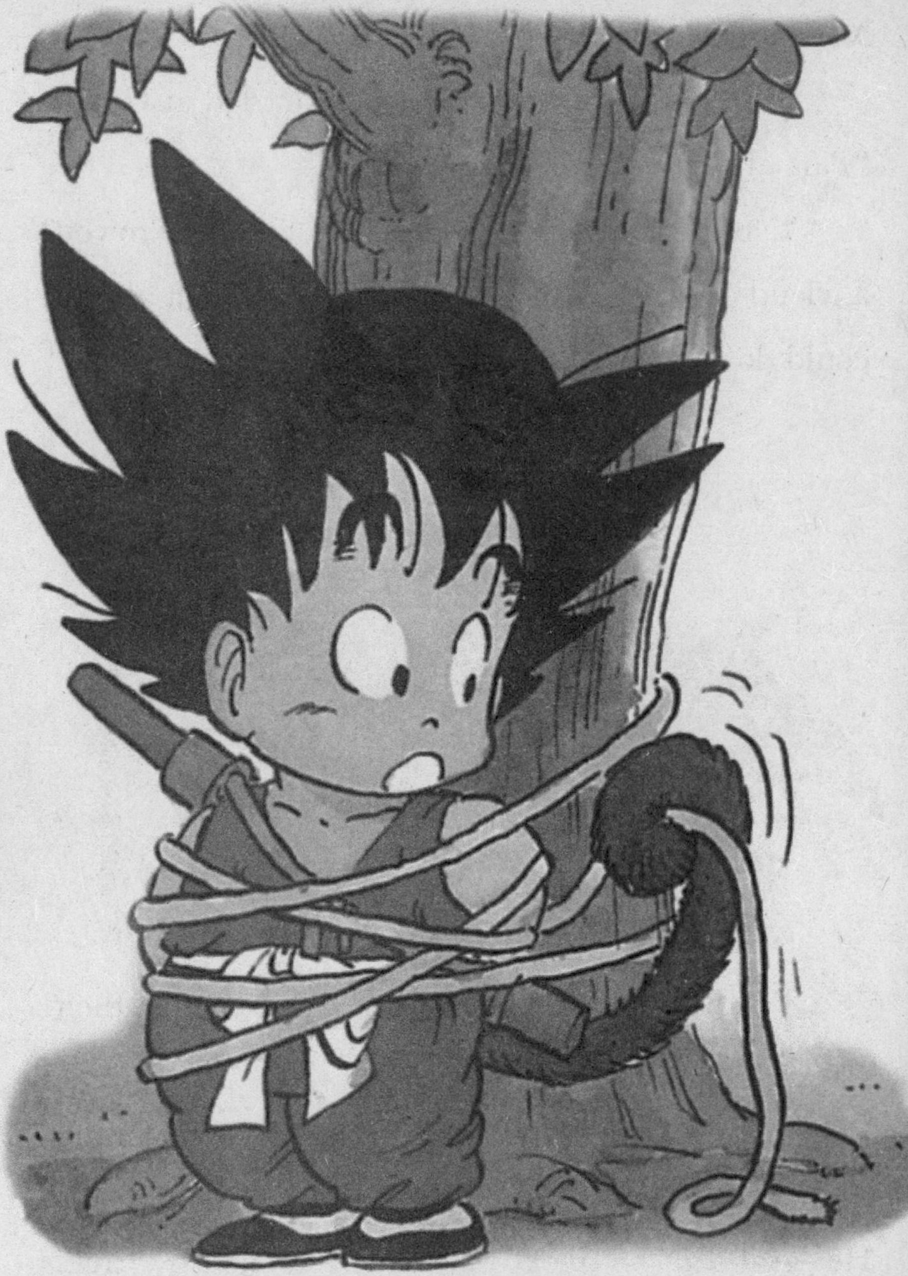

"And there's something she and I have to discuss." The beast nudged Goku toward the tree's trunk. "In private," he snarled, winding the vine around Goku. "Wait right here, okay?"

"Okay," Goku replied, though he couldn't figure out why the dino had bothered tying him to the tree.

The beast took to the sky laughing. "That was too easy. And it's been far too long since I've tasted human flesh!"

"Don't take too long!" Goku called. "I don't like being tied up."

Suddenly, Bulma came to her senses. "Goku! What are you waiting for?!" she yelled. "Rescue me!!"

Huh? thought Goku. *I thought they were friends.*

Goku popped out his tail and untied the vine.

How'm I supposed to rescue her? he wondered, watching the dinosaur vanish into the sky. *Sure would help if I could fly.*

Then he remembered: the motorcycle! He jumped on the seat and tried to remember what Bulma had done to make it go. He pushed the button. He twisted the handlebar. The motorcycle started to run!

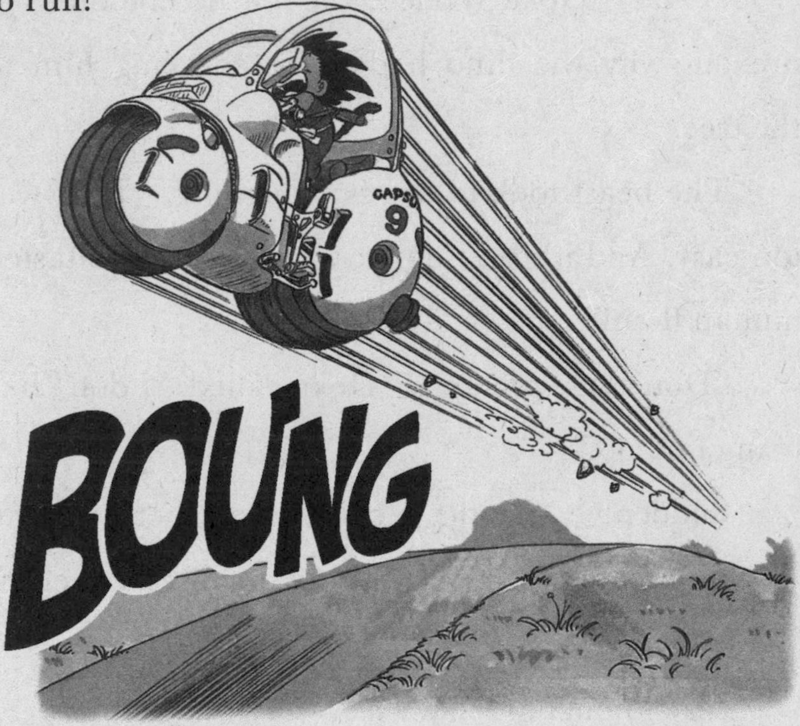
BOUNG
9

Goku drove as fast as he could. He steered the motorcycle onto a hill and roared toward the top. Then—zoom!—the wheels left the ground! He was flying! Straight at the dinosaur!

But before Goku got close enough, the motorcycle began to drop.

"Stupid thing!" Goku said. "I guess I have to do it myself!" He leapt from the bike and whipped out the staff from his back. "All right!" he yelled. "It's Nyoibo time!"

In an instant, the staff was four times longer than Goku himself, long enough for him to take a whack at the dinosaur–BWAK!

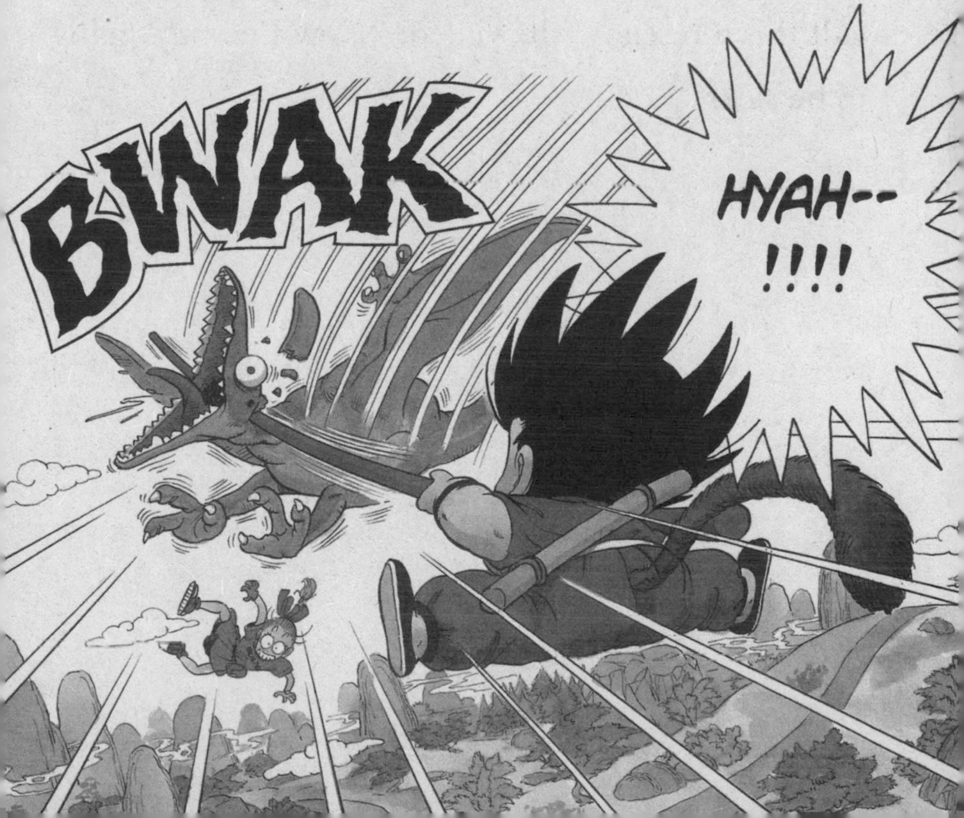
HYAH--
!!!!
BWAK

Stunned, the dinosaur let Bulma go. As she fell, Goku threw his Nyoibo at her. It zipped through one of her sleeves and out the other. The end of the staff jammed into a crack in a high rock and Bulma hung from it like a shirt on a laundry line. Goku landed safely on the ground.

"There!" he called to Bulma. "How's that for a rescue?"

Bulma looked down from the high rock. "You call this a rescue?" she yelled. "Now I'm *really* going to be sick!"

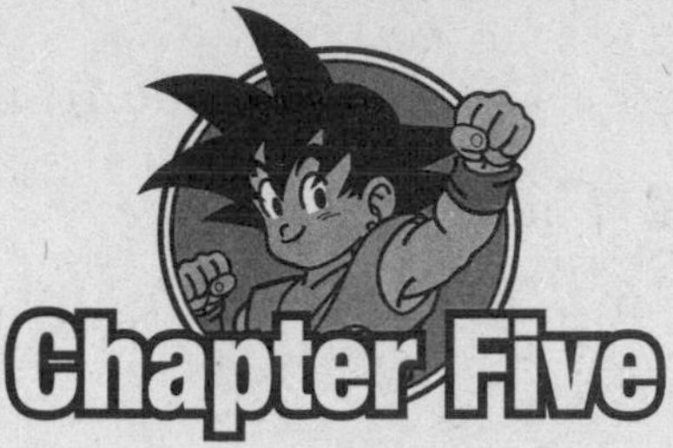
Chapter Five

Chapter Five

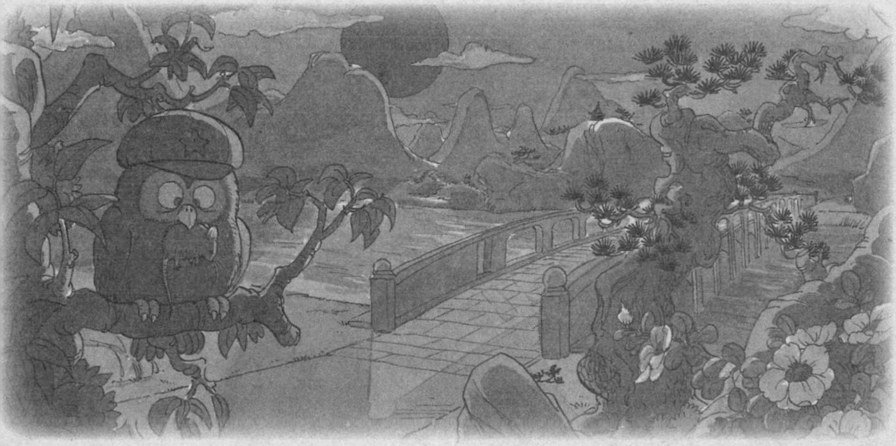

The sun set, and the world grew dark. It was time to stop for the night.

"I'll go find some really soft leaves to sleep on!" Goku offered.

"As if!" Bulma said. "You don't really think I'm going to sleep *outside*, do you?"

She pulled a Hoi-Poi capsule from her case and threw it. Poof! There was house!

"Well?" Bulma smiled. "Still want to sleep on leaves?"

She slid the door open and Goku followed her inside. When she pushed a button lights came on.

"Demon!" Goku cried. "You just turned night into day!"

"Oh give it *up*!" said Bulma, rolling her eyes.

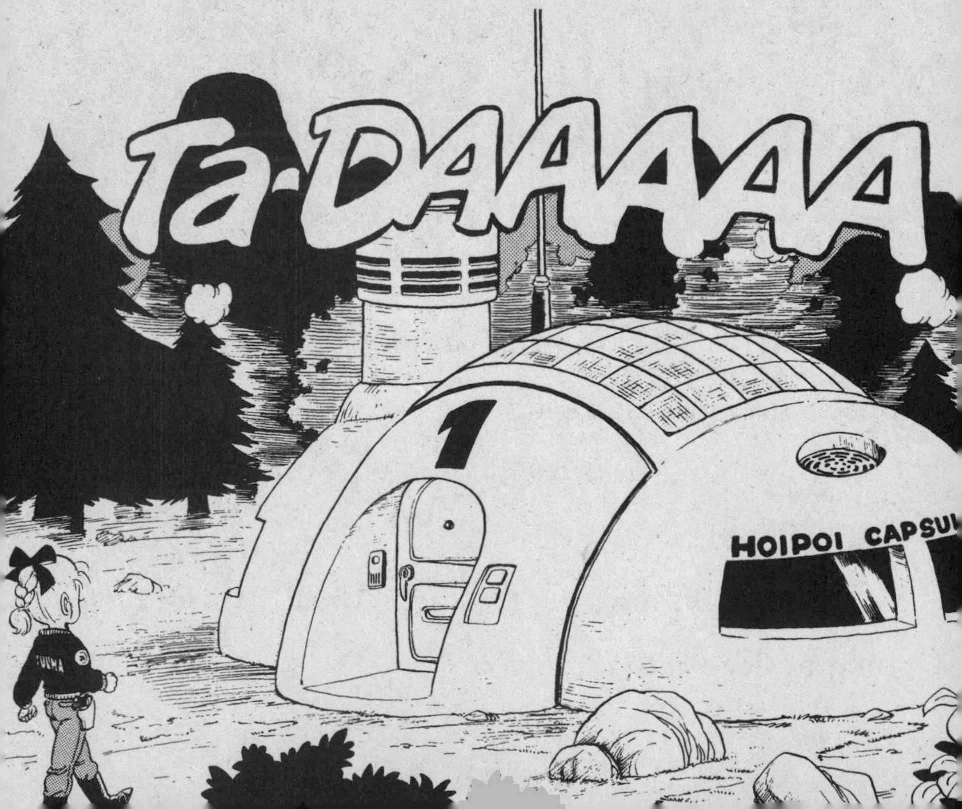
Ta-DAAAAA
1
HOIPOI CAPSU

"Don't you even know about *lights?* You have a lot to learn, monkey-boy. Watch this!"

She pushed another button and a TV came on. Goku jumped back, startled. He stared at the man on the screen. "How'd he get so small?" he asked, tapping the screen with his staff.

Bulma sniffed the air. "Whew!" she gasped. "What's that smell?" She sniffed in Goku's direction. "Oh man!" she said, holding her nose. "You need a bath!"

"A bath?" Goku asked.

"Yes, a bath!" Bulma said, and pushed a button that opened the door to a small bathroom.

"What's a bath?"

"No wonder you stink," Bulma said, dragging him into the bathroom. "Now, take off your clothes, get in this tub, turn the water on, and...*Gaaah!*"

There stood Goku naked as a jaybird.

Bulma covered her eyes. "Get in the tub! Get in the tub!" she cried. As soon as he was in, she turned on the water and squirted in some bubble bath. "You can't just go running around naked in front of people, you know!" she said.

"Sure I can!" he said with a grin. "Watch!"

"No!" Bulma yelled. "Stay in the tub!"

Once there were enough bubbles to cover most of him, Bulma explained all about soap and water, scrub brushes and washcloths.

"Like this?" Goku asked, grabbing a scrub brush with his tail.

Bulma screamed.

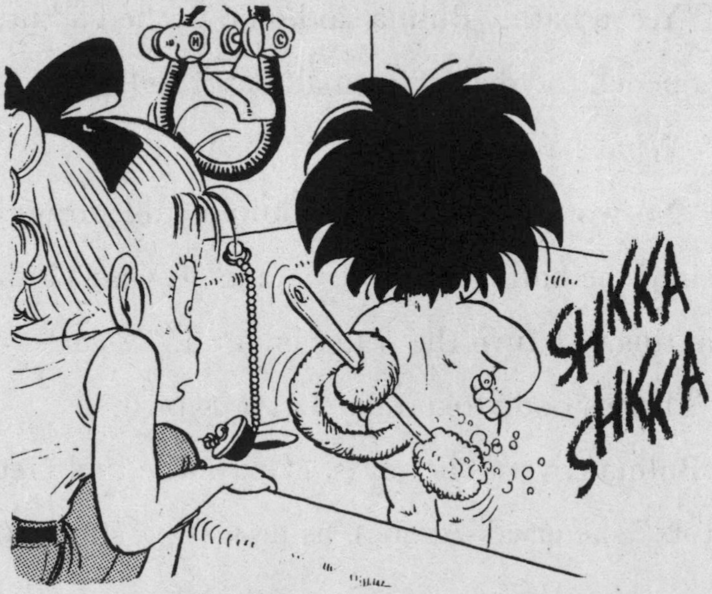
SHKKA
SHKKA

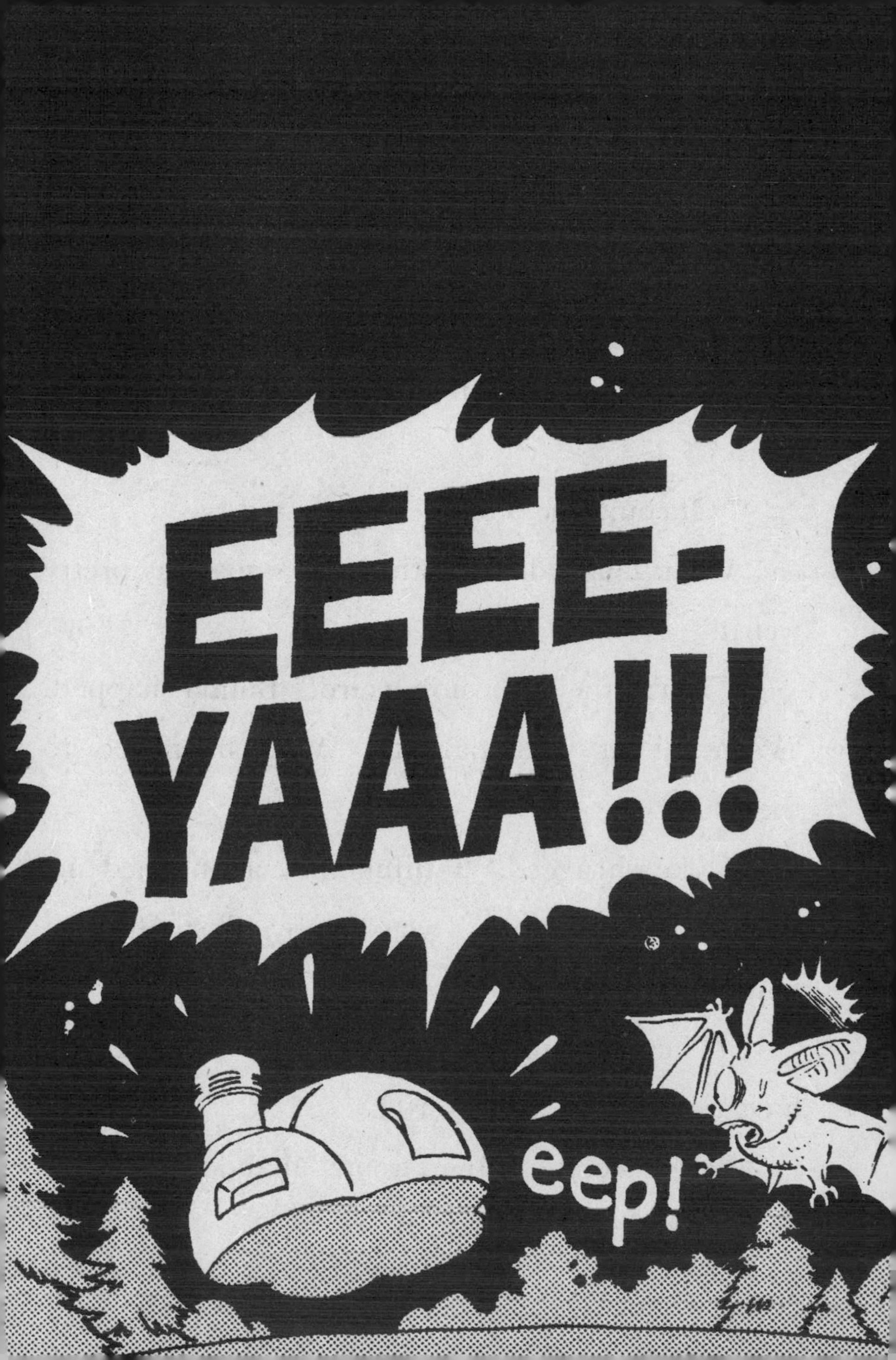
EEEE-YAAA!!!
eep!

"What?" Goku asked, looking around. "Is that dinosaur back?"

"I-it's your tail!" she gasped. "People aren't supposed to have tails!"

"Really?" Goku said, frowning thoughtfully. "Now that you mention it, my grampa didn't have a tail."

"Of course he didn't." Bulma said.

Goku laughed. "But then, Grampa was pretty weird!"

"You're the one who's weird!" Bulma snapped. "What about your parents? What happened to them?"

Goku shrugged. "I think they abandoned me in the mountains when I was a baby. Then Grampa found me."

"They probably abandoned you because you have a tail," Bulma muttered.

"How come your parents abandoned you?" Goku asked.

"Who said I was abandoned?" Bulma snapped. "My father happens to be a very famous scientist. I'm just on summer vacation, and I have only thirty more days to find the rest of the Dragon Balls!

"Take your bath while I make dinner. Tomorrow we have to get started bright and early!"

When Goku came out of the bathroom all clean and dry, Bulma had already put food on the table. It didn't look like the kind of food he was used to, but he was hungry, so he took a bite.

"This is supposed to be *food*?" he said, spitting it out. "This bread stuff is all soft and nasty. And this soup is really bitter!"

"That's coffee!" Bulma said.

Goku headed for the door.

"Hey! Where're you going?" Bulma asked.

"I'm going to get some *real* food!" Goku said.

"What do you mean, *real* food?" Bulma asked, but he was already gone.

"I'm h-o-o-m-e!" Goku called ten minutes later. "And I brought dinner!" There was a wolf slung over his shoulder.

"A *wolf*?!" Bulma cried. "You're going to eat a *wolf*?"

"Well, not plain!" Goku grinned. "I got a centipede for flavor!"

At that, Bulma ran to the bathroom to be sick.

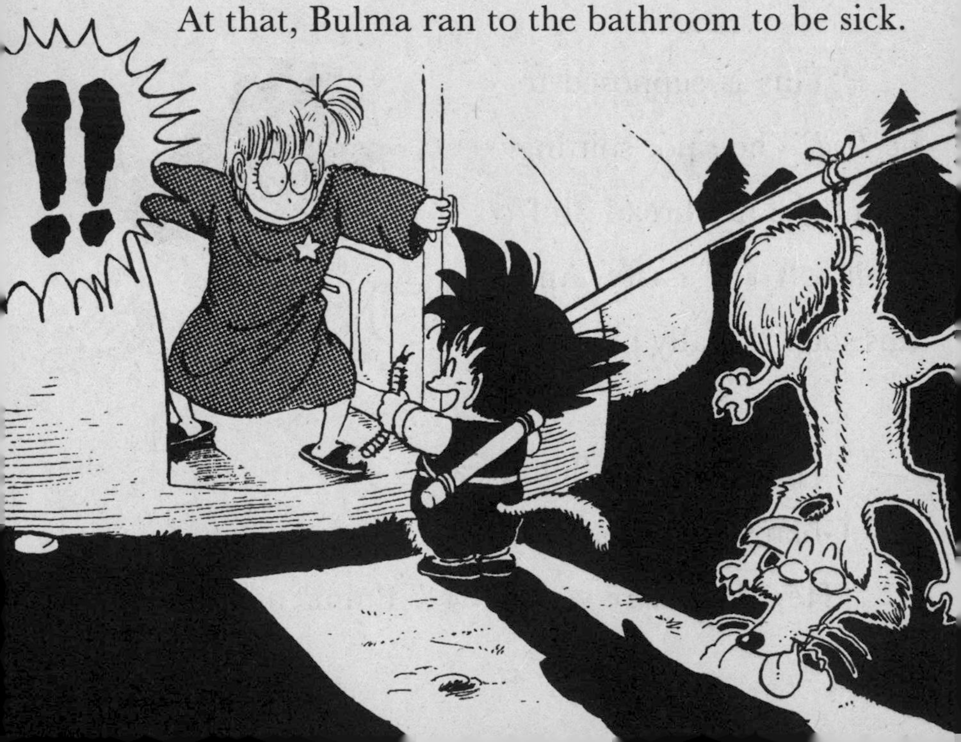
!!

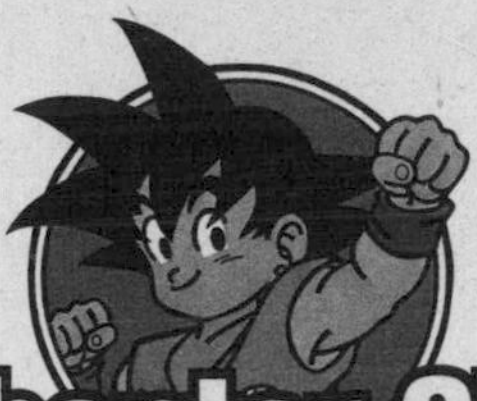

Chapter Six

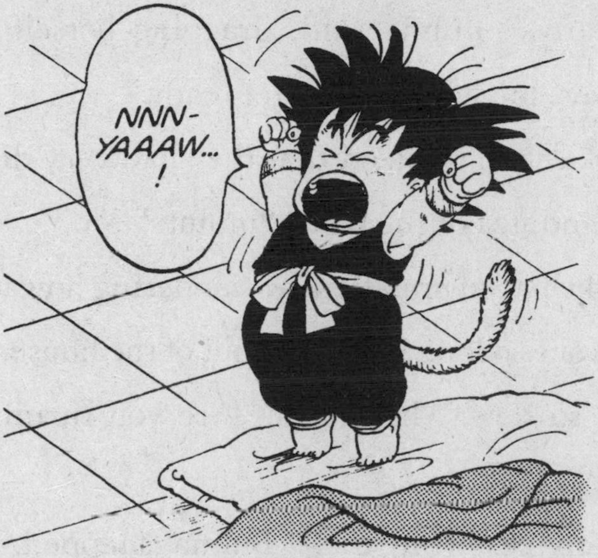
NNN-YAAAW... !

Goku woke at dawn. He had become like the forest animals, sleeping when it was dark and waking when it was light. Bulma, on the other hand, just kept snoring.

"Wake up! Wake up! Wake up!" Goku cried.

"What's wrong?!" Bulma screamed. "What's wrong?!"

"You said you wanted to get started bright and early!" Goku said. "Well, it's early and it's just getting bright!"

"We have very different understandings of the word 'early,'" Bulma said, dragging herself out of bed. "Give me a minute to get ready."

Goku soon realized that they had very different understandings of the word "minute" too.

Goku paced impatiently, wondering how it could take anyone so long just to get out of the house. "Why are you so slow?" he yelled. "Are you turning into a turtle?"

"Stop pestering me!" Bulma snapped. "Why don't you go swing in a tree or something?"

"Great idea!" Goku said. "I need some exercise!"

Goku raced out of the house and found the biggest boulder around. He lifted it, then—"Ho-*ya*!"— squeezed it between his arms. The boulder cracked into a hundred pieces.

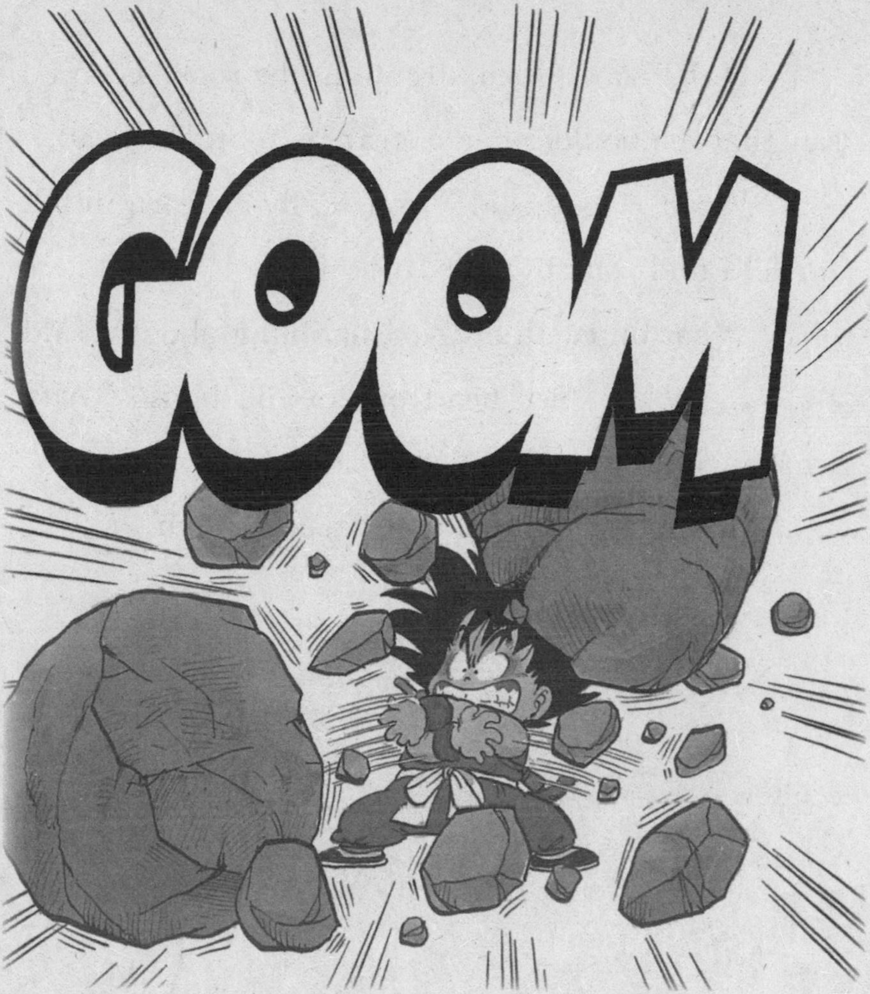
GOOM

"That felt good!" he said. "I need another one!"

He found another boulder, lifted it, and–"Ha-*ya*!"–began to squeeze. "What *are* you doing?!" the boulder yelled.

"Huh?" said Goku, dropping the rock. Then he saw that the boulder had a strange, toothless head.

"Wow!" Goku said. "You really *did* turn into a turtle! I told you not to be so slow."

"What on earth are you babbling about?" said Bulma, sticking her head out of the house. "And what's with the turtle?"

"You mean…it's not you?" asked Goku.

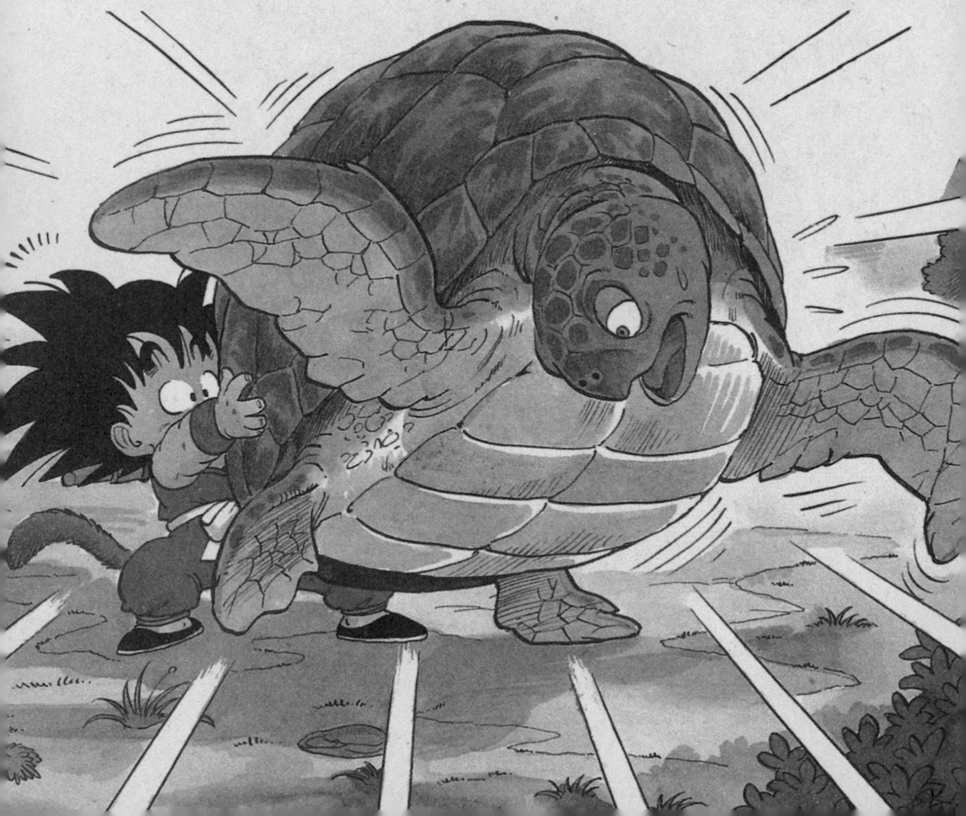

Bulma shot him a dirty look.

"Pardon me for interrupting," the turtle said. "But might I trouble you for a favor?"

"Like what?" Bulma asked.

"Well, you see, I happen to be a turtle…"

"I can *see* that!" Bulma said.

"That's right. A *sea* turtle," the turtle continued. "But I crawled inland and lost my way. I've been wandering for days, trying to find my way back to the sea."

"You've been wandering, all right," Bulma said. "The sea is *miles* from here!"

"Hence the favor," the turtle sighed. "If you could give me directions—and perhaps a bucket of salt water? I'm so terribly thirsty."

"Hey!" said Goku. "Why don't we just take you to the sea?"

"What?!" Bulma cried.

"Oh, I would be so grateful if you could!" the turtle exclaimed.

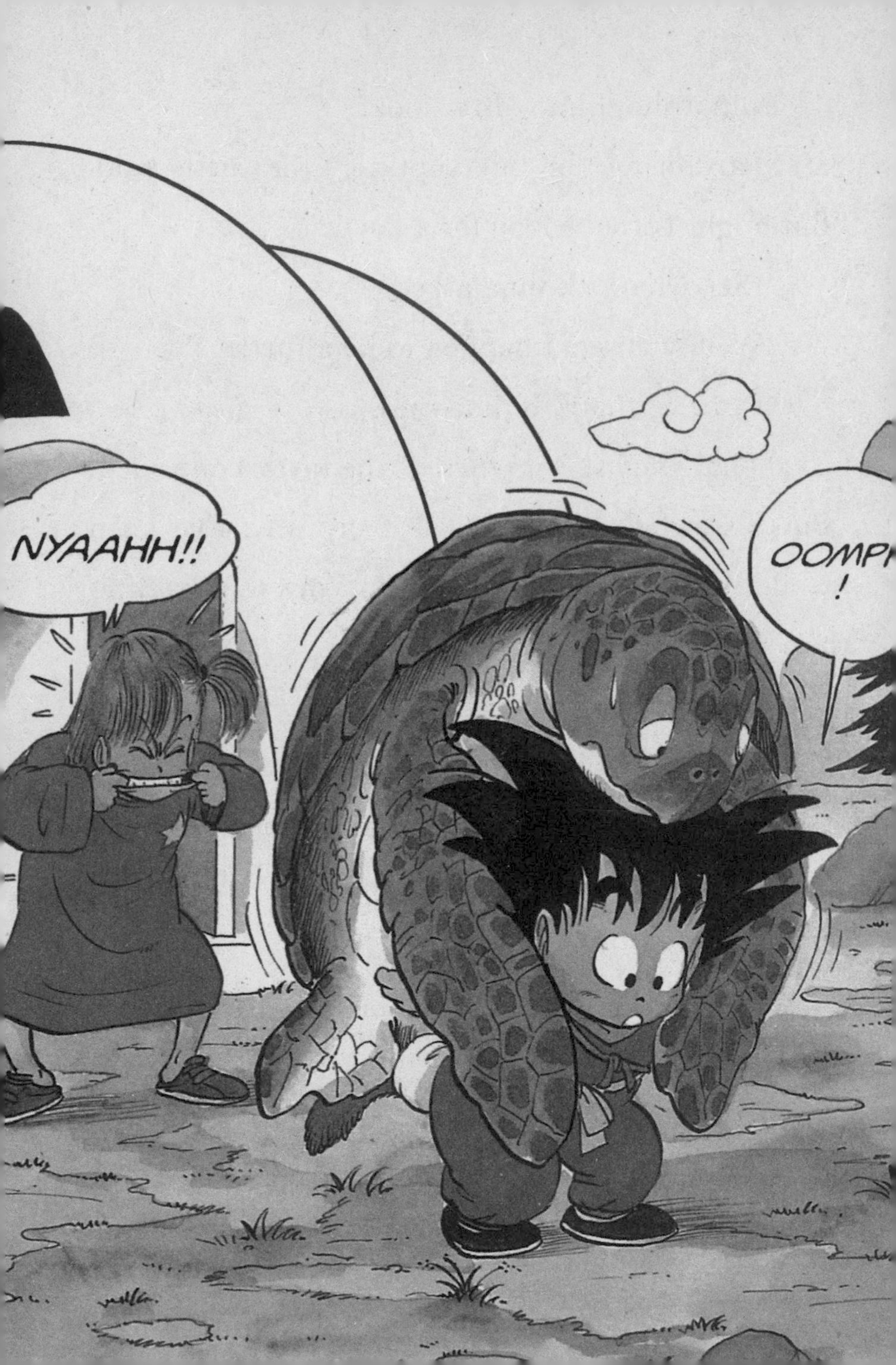
OOMPH
!
NYAAHH!!

"We don't have time for this!" Bulma said. "We have our quest, remember?!"

"Then I'll go without you!" Goku said. "This turtle needs help!" And without another thought he lifted the turtle on his back and walked away.

"I cannot tell you how much this means to me, young sir," the turtle said as he bounced on Goku's back.

"This'll be great exercise!" Goku said excitedly.

"Fine, then!" Bulma said, crossing her arms and watching them go. "Who needs you?!" She watched them walk farther and farther and farther away until they were nearly out of sight.

A breeze blew through the trees. A dinosaur roared in the distance. Something big rustled in the grass.

"Hey! Wait up!" Bulma called after Goku. "You don't even know where you're going! You'll never get there without me!"

A few minutes later, Goku and the turtle heard the roar of Bulma's motorcycle as she came racing toward them.

Chapter Seven

Even carrying a giant turtle on his back, Goku had no trouble keeping up with Bulma on her motorcycle. None of them realized that they were being watched.

"Oh ho," laughed the one doing the watching. "Something tasty this way comes."

Bulma and Goku were traveling at a good pace when suddenly—

"HALT!"—An enormous bear blocked their path. The bear was at least four times Goku's size, and it looked hungry.

"Well, well," drooled the bear. "How did you know that sea turtle is my favorite dish?"

"Ack!" Bulma yelled. "Let him have it, Goku!"

"You mean hit him?" Goku asked.

"No! The turtle!" Bulma yelled. "Let him have the turtle!"

"No way!" Goku said and stuck his tongue out at the bear.

"What's *wrong* with you?" Bulma yelled. "There are a million turtles where that one came from!"

"But *they* didn't ask us for help," Goku said.

"Alright then," the bear said to Goku, "you can be the appetizer to my turtle dinner."

The bear drew his sword high over his head. He brought it down with a mighty roar.

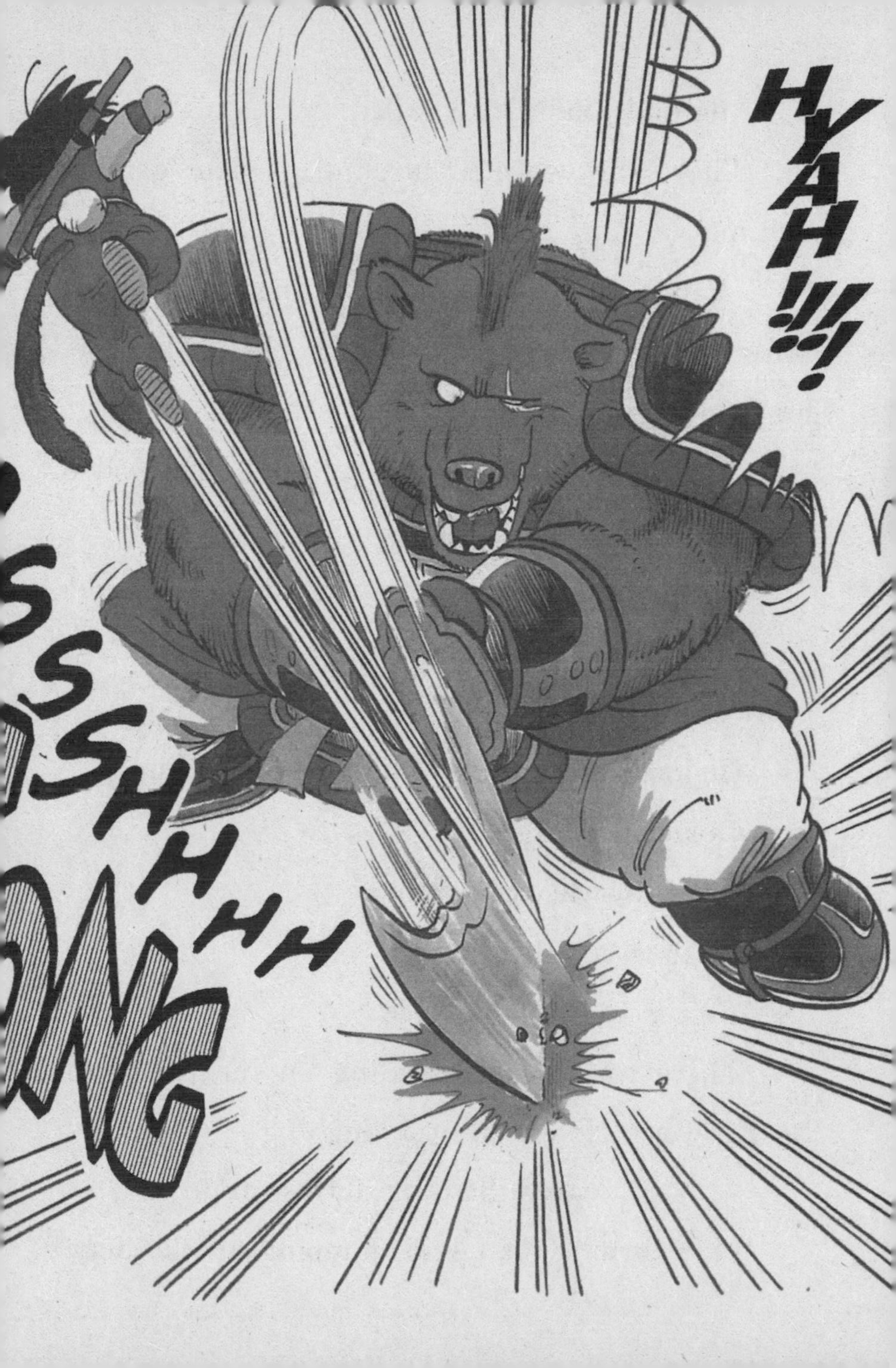
HYAH!!!!
SSSHHHHH

"Behind you!" Goku called.

The bear wheeled around. Goku grinned at him.

"You're a quick little monkey," the bear growled, grinning back. "I just have to be quicker!" He raised his sword again.

"Goku, get on the motorcycle!" Bulma yelled. "Let's get out of here!"

But Goku just stood there, grinning even wider. The bear roared again and whipped his sword down in a vicious slice.

He looked where Goku had been standing.

Goku wasn't there.

The bear wheeled around.

Goku wasn't there either.

"Yoo hoo!" came a voice.

There was Goku, standing on the tip of the bear's sword. He was almost laughing.

"*Arrrgh*!" roared the bear in frustration.

"My turn!" Goku said, jumping on the bear's

snout. "Let's play roshambo!"

"Huh?" said the bear.

"You know!" Goku said. "Scissors..." He made two of his fingers look like scissors. "Paper..." He made his hand flat like a piece of paper. "*Rock*!" he cried. Before the bear knew what was happening, Goku balled his hand into a fist and slammed him between the eyes.

The bear stood for an instant, swaying on his feet. Then he fell heavily backward, landing with a crash.

"Okay, see ya!" Goku called, jumping off the bear's snout.

Bulma and the turtle just stared at him in amazement.

"Hey, Turtle," Goku said, looking the reptile up and down. "Do you really taste that good?"

"N-n-no!" the turtle stammered. "Terrible! Sea turtles taste absolutely dreadful!"

"That's what I thought," laughed Goku. "You don't *look* like you'd taste good!" He lifted the turtle onto his back again.

"When I was fightin' that bear I saw a really wide river just over that hill," said Goku. "An' I'm gettin' thirsty."

"Wide river?" asked the turtle. "You don't mean...you can't mean..." At that moment they reached the top of the hill.

"It's the sea!" cried the turtle. "You've done it, lad! You've brought me home!"

"Wow," Goku said, looking at the sea. "That's

a lotta water for you to swim around in!"

"Young man, I cannot begin to thank you for what you've done," the turtle said. "Such generosity deserves a reward! Please wait right here!" The turtle plunged into the water and disappeared under the waves.

"Oh well," Bulma sighed, sitting on the sand. "I guess we can wait around for a reward."

"Hey!" Goku sputtered. "Who put salt in this water?"

Bulma didn't even try to explain. She was too busy watching something coming toward them in the water. "Is that...the turtle?" she asked.

Goku looked. "Yeah," he said. "But he's got something on his back. It must be the reward!"

"Is it a giant pearl?" Bulma asked. "A priceless ancient statue?"

"Nuh-uh," Goku said, squinting. "It's an old man!"

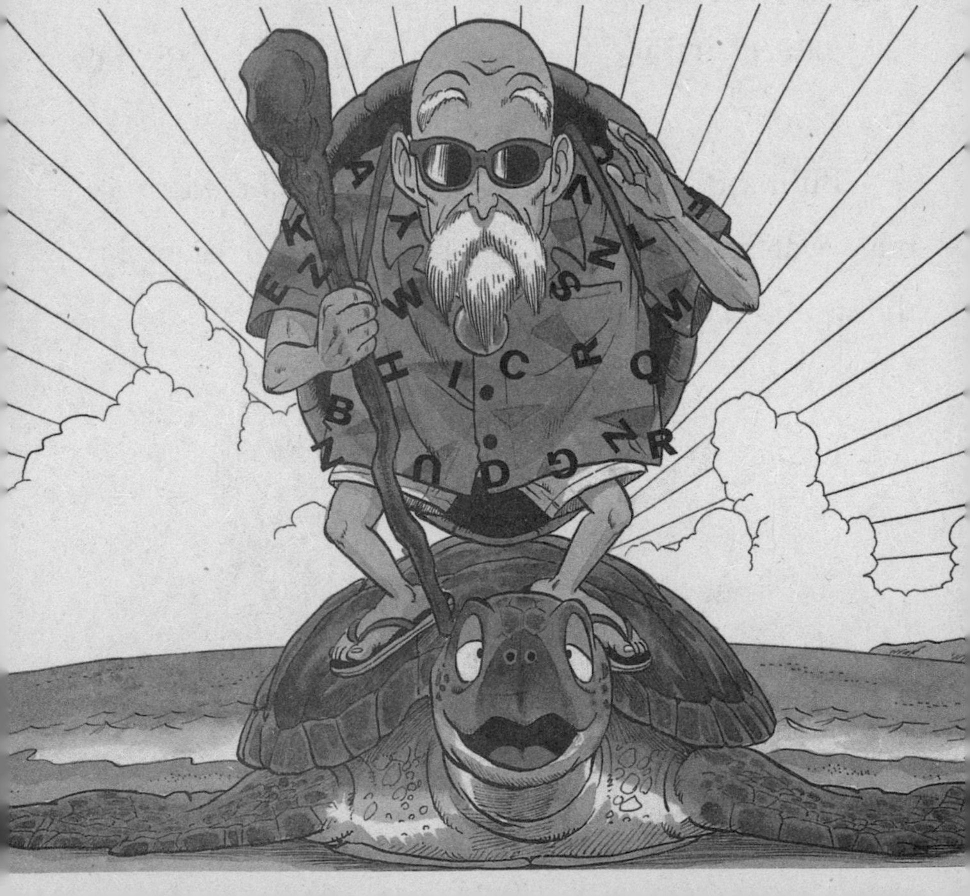

Chapter Eight

"Our reward is an old man?" Bulma asked. She did not look happy.

"Howdy, young'uns!" the old man called.

"Who're you?" asked Goku.

"Who am I?" the old man said, taking a dramatic pause. "I am the invincible Master Roshi! Also known as the Turtle Hermit."

Slowly, carefully, the invincible master climbed down from the turtle's back. He walked with the help of a big stick. "I hear you two were very kind to my turtley friend here."

"Actually," said the turtle, "it was only the lad."

"Hey! That's not fair!" Bulma yelled.

"Alright, m'boy," Master Roshi said to Goku, "I will give you the finest gift imaginable! I summon... the immortal phoenix!"

He jabbed his stick at the sky.

Nothing happened.

"Um...sir?" the turtle whispered. "If you'll recall that unpleasantness with the spoiled birdseed..."

"Oh, right!" the hermit said, clearing his throat. "So sad when we lost the poor feller. Well, hmm. Oh, wait! I've got it! Even better than the phoenix! I summon...*Kinto'un*!"

He jabbed his stick into the sky again. This time something came zooming toward them.

"It's...a *cloud*?!" Bulma gasped.

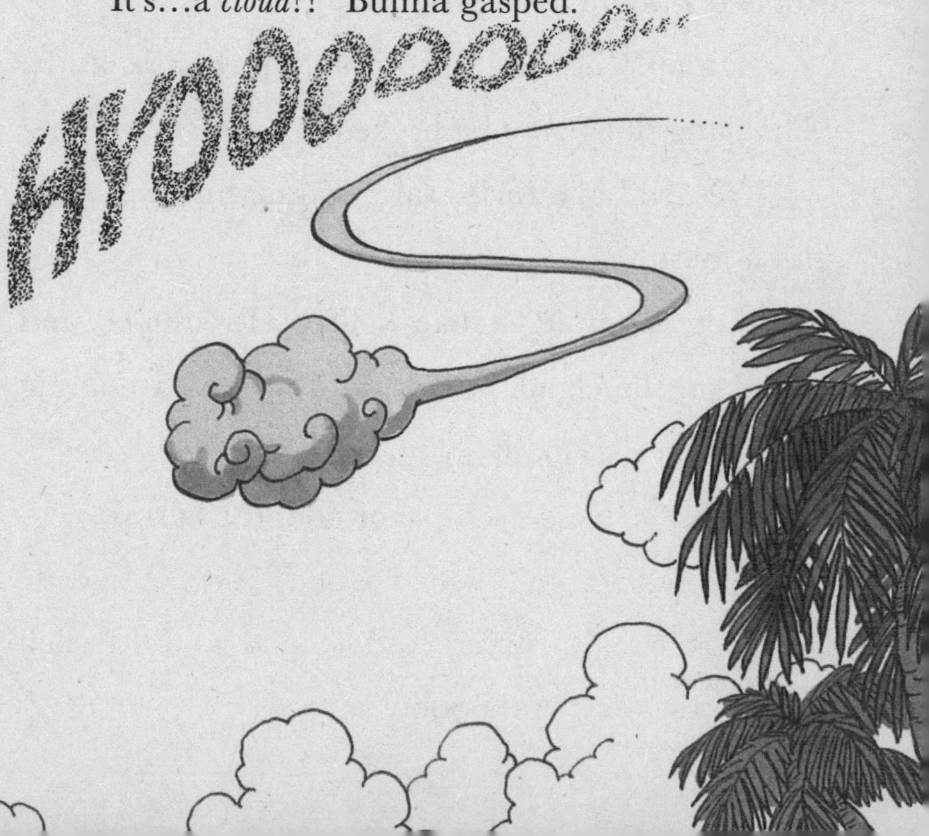
HYOOOOOOO...

"Is that for me?" Goku asked.

"That's for you!" Master Roshi said.

"How do I *eat* it?" Goku asked.

"You don't eat a magic cloud!" the hermit said. "You ride it! But here's the thing: no one can ride Kinto'un unless he is truly pure of heart. Watch me!"

Master Roshi jumped onto the cloud. And dropped straight through.

"Hmph," he grumbled, rubbing his backside. "The dang thing *must* be broken!"

"Yes, sir," the turtle said, rolling his eyes. "I'm sure it must be."

"Let *me* try it!" Goku yelled. He jumped and landed on the cloud. It held him up like a floating floor. "I'm on a cloud!" he gasped. "I'm on a *cloud*!"

"Must've fixed itself," muttered the hermit.

"Go, cloud, go!" yelled Goku, and the speedy puff took off! It curved and looped and wheeled through the air. "Wahooooo!"

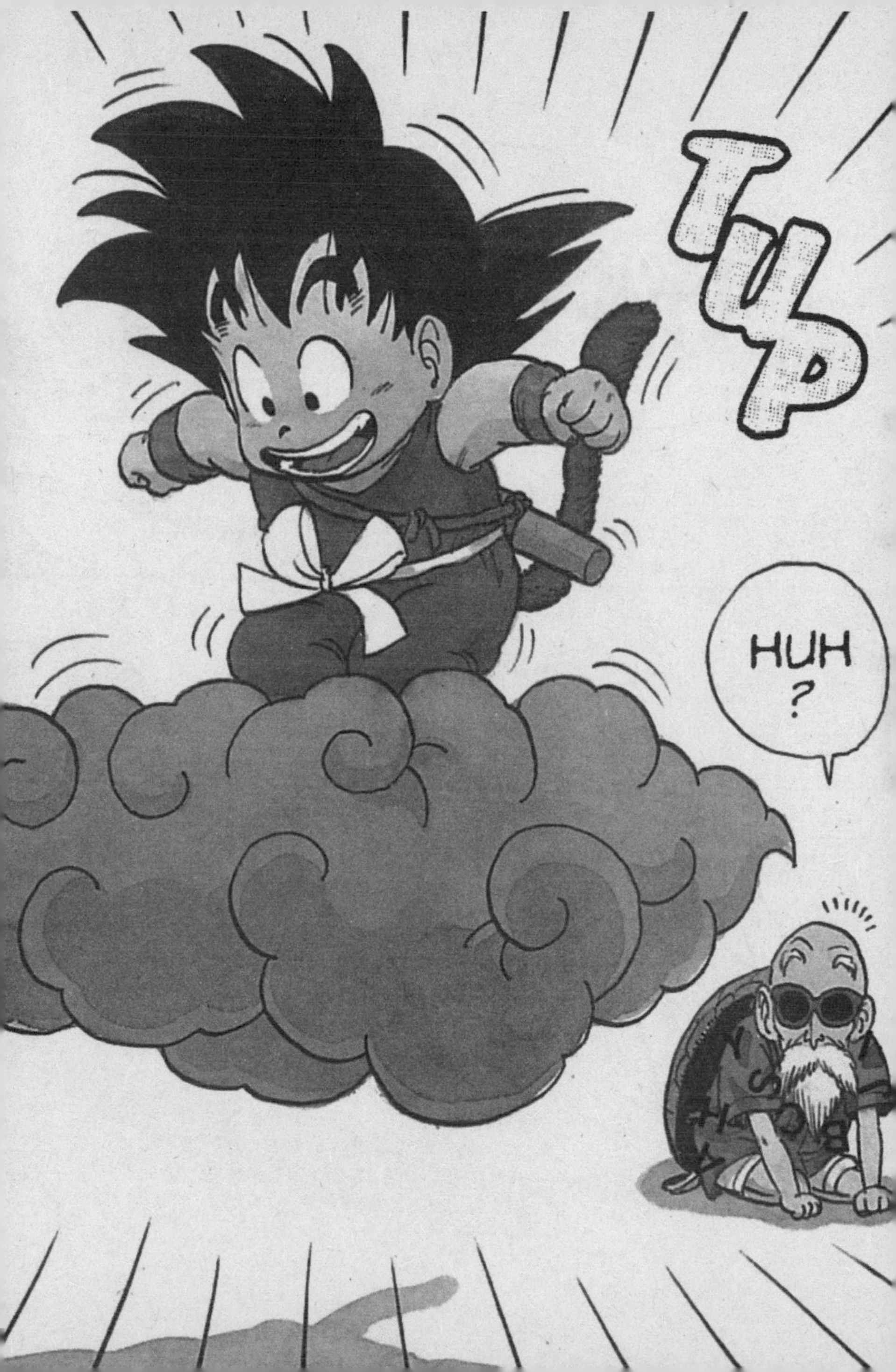
TUP
HUH?

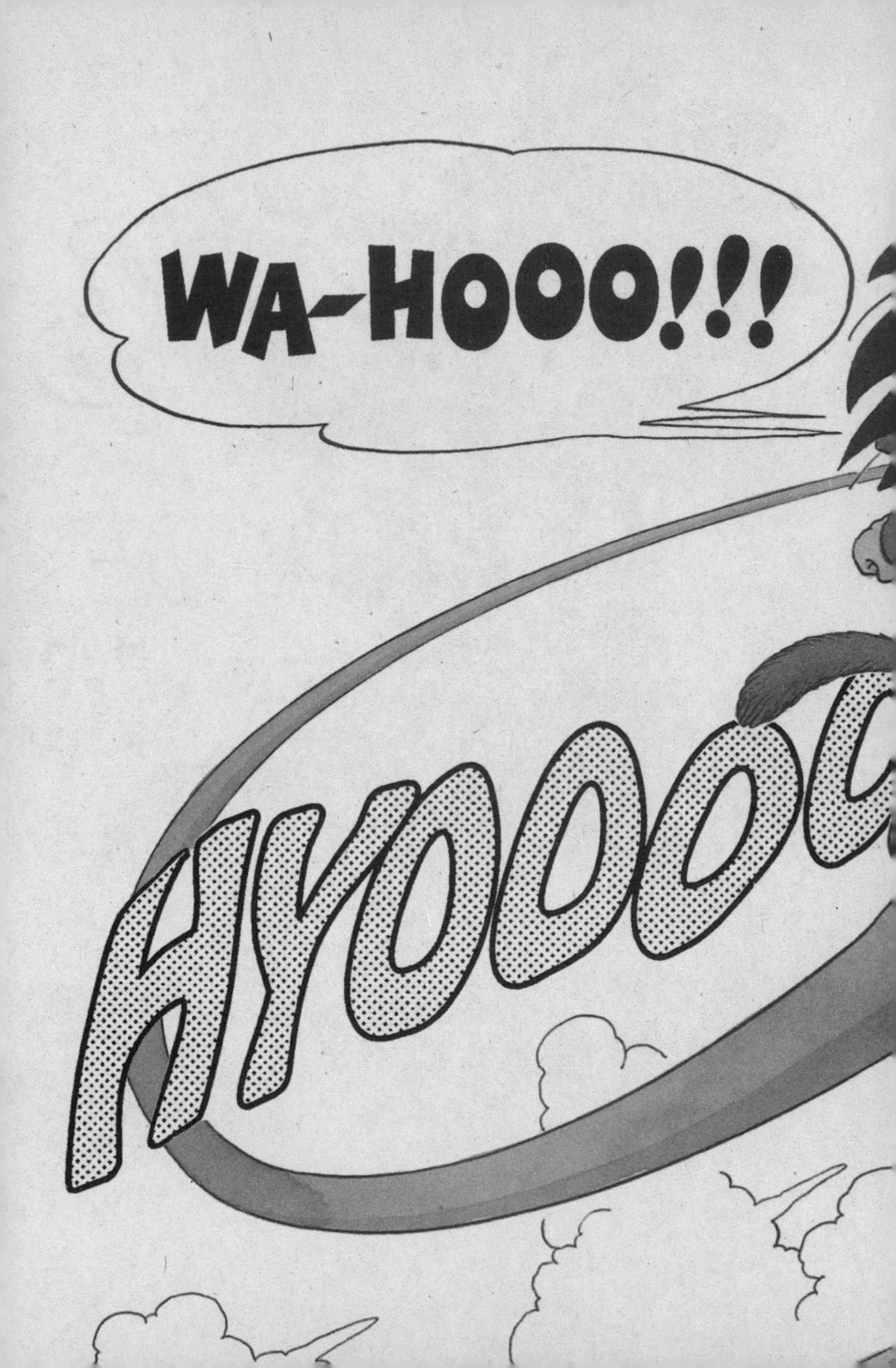
WA-HOOOO!!!
HYOOOO

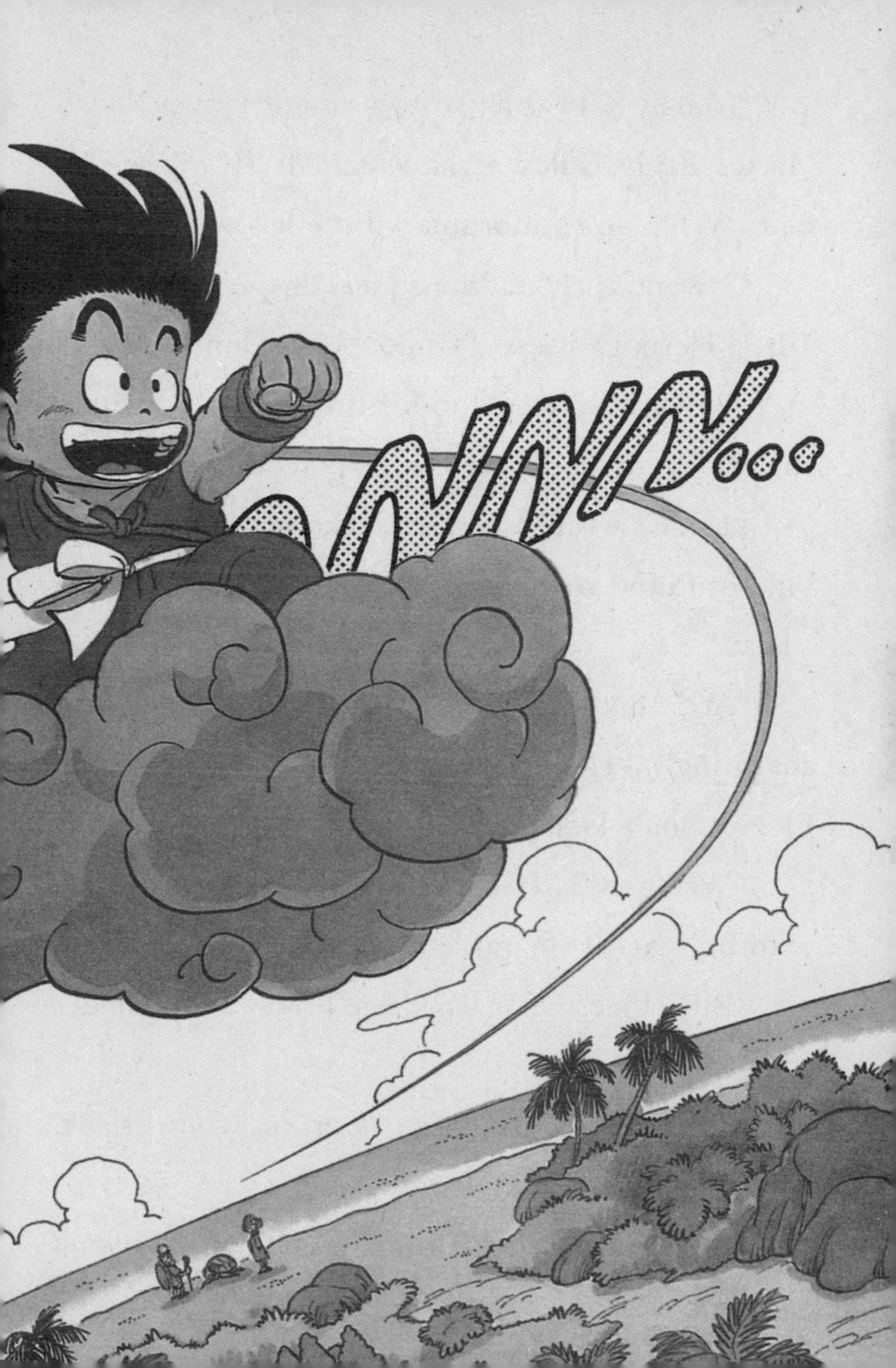
NNN...

"You fly Kinto'un like it was made for you, boy!" Master Roshi called as he watched. To himself he said, "What an extraordinary little fellow."

"I want one!" Bulma squealed, pulling on the Turtle Hermit's sleeve. "Gimme one! Gimme one!"

The hermit turned to his turtle friend. "Didn't you tell me that only the boy helped you?"

"I don't wish to be rude," the turtle said. "But I'm afraid the young lady did suggest feeding me to a bear."

"Aw, that was just a joke!" Bulma laughed charmingly. "How 'bout this. If you give me a cloud, I'll give you a kiss."

"Well now," Master Roshi said and leaned closer to Bulma. "If you put it *that* way…"

"Sir! Honestly!" gasped the turtle. "No wonder you couldn't ride Kinto'un!"

Master Roshi snorted. "Cut me some slack, Leatherback! It's just one little kiss!"

But Bulma wasn't thinking about the cloud

anymore. When the hermit had leaned close to her, she noticed something around his neck. It was a necklace—with a crystal ball hanging from it. Three stars glowed inside.

"A Dragon Ball!" Bulma gasped. "You have *Sanshinchu!*"

"This old thing?" the hermit asked. "I found this on the ocean floor...oh, about a hundred years ago."

Bulma grabbed the ball and yelled: "I want it! I want it!"

"Don't tell me it's worth somethin'!"

Goku came zooming down on his cloud. "What are you yelling about, Bulma?"

"The old-timer's giving me a Dragon Ball!" Bulma yelled.

"Now wait just a minute," Master Roshi said. "I never said–"

"Hey, Turtle Guy?" Goku called. "Bulma an' I are trying to find all the Dragon Balls, and it sure would be nice if we could have this one. You can even have the cloud back if Bulma can have this ball."

Master Roshi looked as though he wanted to argue, but with the turtle watching him, and Bulma watching him, and Goku being so noble, he just couldn't do it.

"My boy," he said, "now I see why you're able to ride Kinto'un. Keep the cloud. And you, young lady, take this Dragon Ball as my gift."

"Oh, thank you!" Bulma squealed. She snatched the crystal ball from his hand and shoved it in her pack before the hermit had a chance to change his mind.

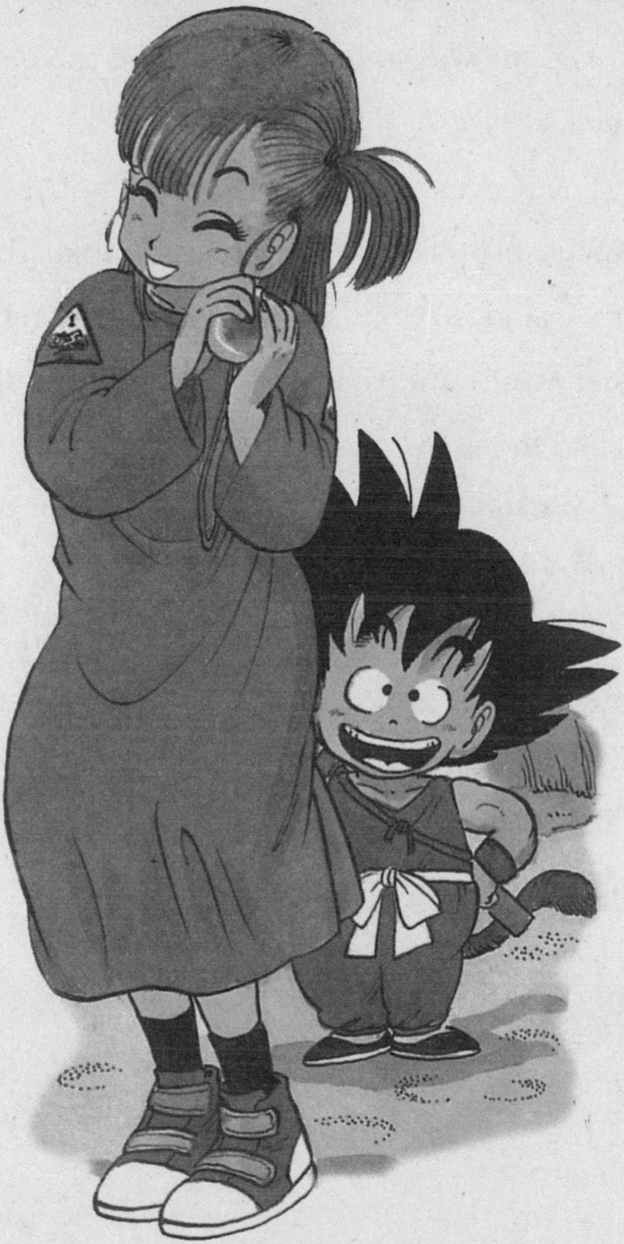

"Now I have four! I'm over halfway there!"

And she was so happy she kissed the old man on the cheek.

Then everyone said their goodbyes. Bulma climbed onto her motorcycle and Goku turned his magic cloud so that he was flying alongside her. Master Roshi and the turtle stood by the shore and watched them go.

"You got your kiss after all, didn't you, sir?" smiled the turtle.

"You know," sighed the hermit, "on days like today, it's good to be alive."

They kept watching until Bulma and Goku disappeared into the distance, off on their quest to find the last three Dragon Balls.

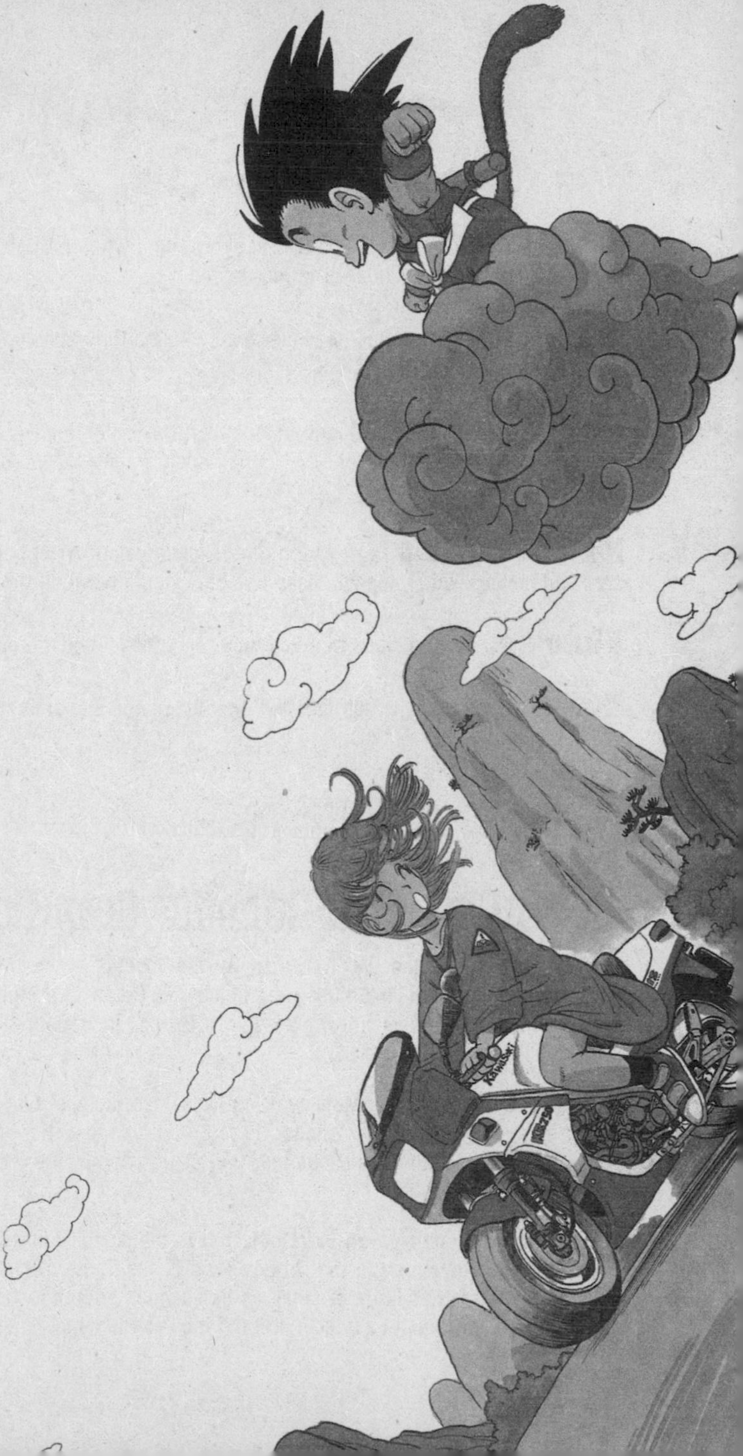

Glossary

Dragon Ball: one of seven mythical orbs that when brought together have the power to summon a wish-granting dragon

Dragon Radar: a machine invented by Bulma that picks up and tracks the energy of the Dragon Balls

Fist of Roshambo: one of Goku's favorite fighting moves in which he uses the hand formations from the game "Rock, Paper, Scissors" to overpower his opponent

Hoi-Poi Capsule: a tiny tube that holds any number of objects—including cars and houses—and releases these objects when thrown on the ground

Kinto'un: a flying cloud that will only carry those who are pure of heart

Nyoibo: Goku's magic fighting staff that lengthens on command

A Note About the Monkey King

The *Dragon Ball* series was inspired by the legend of the Monkey King, a mischievous character in Chinese mythology. In China, the Monkey King (who is an actual monkey) is known as Sun Wukong. In Japan, he is known as Son Goku.

According to legend, the Monkey King was incredibly strong and fast, and could somersault great distances through the clouds. He could transform into 72 different animals and objects, and could change the hairs on his body into thousands more.

Sun Wukong also carried an extremely heavy magic rod known as *Ruyi Jingu Bang* that once belonged to the Dragon King of the Eastern Seas. Sun Wukong could make the rod as large or small as he wished. When he wasn't using it, he made the rod as small as a needle and hid it behind his ear.

About the Authors

Akira Toriyama
Original Creator of the *Dragon Ball* Manga

Artist/writer Akira Toriyama burst onto the manga (Japanese comics) scene in 1980, with the wildly popular *Dr. Slump*, a science fiction comedy about the adventures of a mad scientist and his android daughter. In 1984 he created the beloved series *Dragon Ball,* which has been translated into many languages, and, as a series, has sold over 150 million copies in Japan. Toriyama-san lives with his family in Japan.

Gerard Jones
Dragon Ball Chapter Book Author

Gerard Jones has been adapting Japanese manga for English-speaking audiences since 1989, including the entire run of *Dragon Ball* comics for VIZ Media and the *Pokémon* comic strip for Creators Syndicate (reprinted by VIZ as *Pikachu Meets the Press*). He has also written hundreds of original comic books for Marvel, DC, and other publishers, and he is the author of several books on popular culture and children's media, including *Killing Monsters* and the Eisner Award-winning *Men of Tomorrow.* He lives in San Francisco with his wife and son, where he works and teaches at the San Francisco Writers Grotto.

Coming Soon...

Book Two
DRAGON BALLS IN DANGER!

There's something fishy–or piggy, perhaps?–about the deserted town Bulma and Goku travel to next. But it's home to a Dragon Ball, so our heroes charge ahead. Just when it seems they're living high on the hog, Goku and Bulma cross paths with Yamcha and Pu'ar, the deadly duo of the desert. Is this the end of the quest? Has the bacon hit the pan? Find out in book two of *Dragon Ball!*

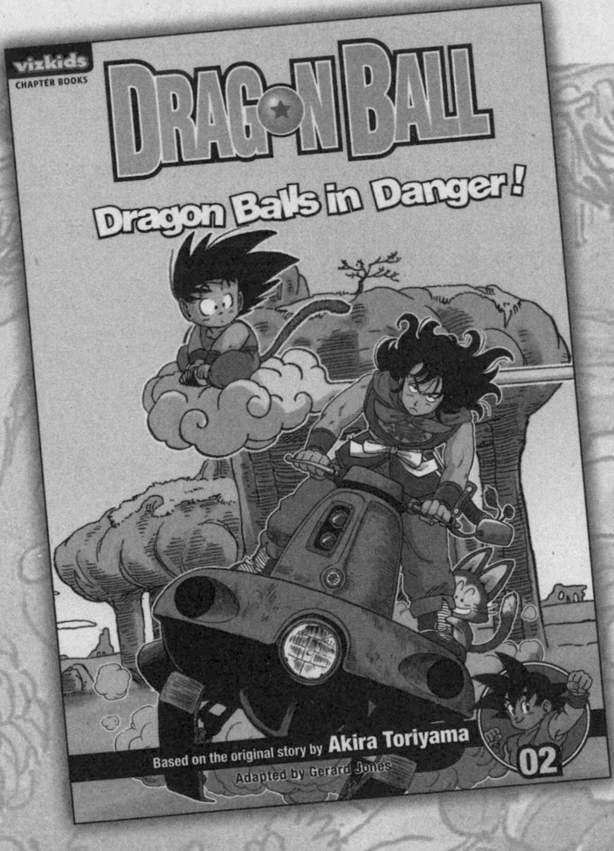
vizkids
CHAPTER BOOKS
DRAGON BALL
Dragon Balls in Danger!
Based on the original story by Akira Toriyama
Adapted by Gerard Jones
02